Introduction by Eileen Myles

This Dead Book

I've been reading Nate Lippens for years. I think this is the third time I've read *My Dead Book* and I'm finally getting a grip on what kind of machine his writing is. I think it's a poetic instrument and also some kind of natural phenomena. I went to Joshua Tree one night in the aughts with a gang of people to see the Perseids. I've been thinking about that. We had sleeping bags and some people had drinks and their drugs of choice and then we all laid down flat looking up the sky waiting for the show. There wasn't much. Like almost nothing. There's one. And then in maybe about seven minutes another. Then another one. And nothing for a while. Then wham and all of the sudden we were screaming, giddy as kids because we were getting inundated with meteors making the sky like this crazy vibing net and we were ancient people animals lying there looking up in naked awe. It was the best. Start to finish I think that's what Nate Lippens has done. Let me lay it out here. *My Dead Book* starts off with a fairly sentimental recitation, a recollection of one of his dead friends from the past. And then another one. I mean of course I like the way he writes. It's clean, it's fairly direct, and conceptually I am reminded of how practical friendship is to a lost child which this narrator definitely is. If you don't know who you are then you make yourself up with bits and pieces of your friends. And losing them means continually losing yourself who never existed except what you got from them and what's constant in these evocations and recollections is the trashy elegance, swarming and specific bravado of a collection of souls who are lost and living antithetical to the values of the culture itself. Young rent boys and old rent boys and the people who collect them. We have books of course that are memoirs by particular people living in particular times but *My Dead Book* will have none of that. These are no ones mostly. Self-declared. It's a midwestern book. Going to New York or LA to trick, even living there for a while but always coming back. Maybe there's one kind of someone but he doesn't value that. And it turns out he's invented. He's mostly me, Nate said. So we're on the fringe, the fringe of the fringe. So what we have is loss and a compounding of loss, more and more. People age out, bodies get found in the river. People jump in the river. The cup spilleth over. So what's the story. It's a rhythmic trick. Like poetry. Like god is. And a queer one. His narrator tells about Gore Vidal saying that there are no homosexual people, only homosexual acts. So wise in a late-night

Copyright © 2024 Nate Lippens

All rights reserved. No part of this book may be reproduced, stored in a retrieval system, or transmitted by any means, electronic, mechanical, photocopying, recording, or otherwise, without prior permission of the publisher.

Published by Semiotext(e)
PO BOX 629, South Pasadena, CA 91031
www.semiotexte.com

Cover image: Caption: Mark Morrisroe, *Ramsey, Lake Oswego*, 1988
C-print, negative sandwich, 20 x 16 inches. © The Estate of Mark Morrisroe
(Ringier Collection) at Fotomuseum Winterthur

Design: Hedi El Kholti
ISBN: 978-1-63590-214-3

10 9 8 7 6 5 4 3 2 1

Printed and bound in the United States of America.
Distributed by the MIT Press, Cambridge, MA, and London, England.

MY DEAD BOOK

Nate Lippens

Introduction by Eileen Myles

Semiotext(e)

This book is dedicated in loving memory to
my brother Jamie Lippens

talk-show way (and Nate is not from that generation [mine] who stayed up late to see Truman Capote and Oscar Levant and Gore Vidal preen and pontificate on swivel chairs, but he's entirely *of* it and Oscar Wilde too, definitely the Oscar Wilde of *De Profundis* but funnier) but the joke I want is how our narrator finds that quote funny because *Gore Vidal* was such a faggot. Rich as he was and toney and all he nonetheless handed them that joke. He was one of the boys. So he knew he'd be laughed at when he left the room or when the teevee went off for the night. So imagine reality being that place then. So we retreat into language here. Some of the jokes are just quietly squeezing the repetition. Almost with your fingertips. *If money weren't a factor* somebody, a friend with money, begins a speech. What follows is a very conversational sequence of if-money-weren't-a-factors but thinky, inside oneself. Which is also one of the main soundstages here. The narrator can't sleep so he's prone to long conversations with himself. If money weren't a factor he asks finally (alone in bed) *would we even know each other?* It's a quiet laugh followed by further critique of the wealthier friend but he has displayed his sword, his wit so we roll along for the next skein of thoughts. Nate takes huge risks with our capacity to suffer with him. And I *like* being pushed to that edge which is like watching your single mom clean the house and never knowing (it might take forever) when she is going to say something disarmingly filthy or just informative—something you'd never *known* about her before.

Of his class of boys Nate Lippens tells us:

> We remembered social workers, outreach volunteers, and youth counselors with their advice, programs, groups, condoms, free anonymous screenings, and clean syringes. They trained us to be vigilant. No exceptions. They saved our lives and taught us to trust no one.

It's a revelation. These dark comedians were "built" in so many ways. By social programs that saw everything but them. These are the kids who had the shit kicked out of them in school, whose dads beat them up for being fags— *Dear officer Krupke fuck you*—but gay. The inside strikes back with a ton of young and not-so-young death. Thud, then everyone returning for encores throughout the text while the bodies keep landing on the deck like fish. Thump. And that's the story.

There's no rules when you're not telling a story but stories. For me that's the most redemptive thing of all. And because the narrator always loved Shane, perhaps the most recurring burnished tragic figure here, he ends a passage explaining that he wanted to save him with a kind of *Diamond Dogs* flourish:

I pictured us like salamanders, emerging from the fire with bright iridescent scales. Always the "just before" creates the very swirl of this. I imagine such lines bursting forth from hours of listening to music high for hours, and beauty and excess stepping out to dance just like humor always puts a stop to things and gets us out of the room. As I read *My Dead Book* again I was increasingly in awe at Nate's timing and intuition. He was a poet first before anything else and you can smell it here. Most machinically, his bits and pieces are generally just a third of a page, a procession of them. This is a book full of asterisks for sure. Just when we've hit bottom with a character's absolute inability to have intimacy with anyone other than his listening friend (and including him) the story races off to consider a world where "all the people who called 'us' bitter in the '90s are now"—guess!?—"at the Whitney's David Wojnarowicz exhibit." Point being they would eat our dead bodies if we were famous. Turned out like this, the despair that floods this book like an abandoned car feels more like everybody's problem and it is.

Humor is a kind of disordering, like 10, 9, 8, 7, *3!* and *3* tears a hole in your expectation and you crawl out laughing from a trap. Sometimes it's ta-dum, sometimes a line noodles in like the moment when he's talking about a show of matchbooks from "now-defunct gay bars and sex clubs." His tone slightly shifts maybe lowers before explaining that the show refers to "a time that is an intermittent blinking on some abandoned shore, maybe." I love the *maybe*. A whole era could be vast as in a movie about it, or infinitesimal like a kind of distant unforgettable light. But honestly it's almost more than the beauty of the line, its *noodling*, its refusal to be major as another way of honoring what's past. We were and now we are not. That's all it means to say. It's antimonumental. I feel I'm in danger of saying things I've said before, swooping Nate's work into a wave of praise for things I've categorized before. If he's related to that he shines most as the most uncategorizable, a poet of adamantine failure who while he's experiencing the heft of his own declaration teases himself and us with vows of love, pledges to specific beauties, rages against conformities of comfort in relation to wealth and ideas and who's declared valuable by "the community" (a word which he sneers at, delightedly) that wants to embellish our gay or queer love with the cozy and warm fragrance of home (and—*at last*—acceptance).

The spikey poetic homelessness of *My Dead Book* is in relation to a devotion to not fitting in, not anywhere ever. I haven't read this yet before, not anywhere at all, though he's moved by a literature I know that is never fiction or nonfiction but poetic fact unravelled with unparalleled and sidestepping skill.

Whatever his truth is he's willing to die for it, woulda, but didn't. And there's one final effect which I've got to mention which is that once I've gotten used to the erratic flicker of his prose, the effects that randomly lighten his dead load, as the book comes to its final curve and it feels a bit like the narrator is a survivor after all and is mourning his loves and his own life and his family in recollection, what I've experienced in this book is formal somehow, the lights begin to stay and the final passage is bright as hell like one star stayed, yup, and got us home as well. It says hello. And man, can you write.

MY DEAD BOOK

1

My dead friends are back. I lie in bed at night and see them.

* * *

It was the summer Jeffrey Dahmer was arrested and his horrific murders were splashed across the newspapers. Another Wisconsin serial killer. Keenan and I lived in the upstairs flat of a house on North Fratney by the school. Kids on recess screamed through our morning haze. Keenan worked a few hotels downtown and I stuck to porn arcades and parking lots. He only had one rule: no heroin. Booze and coke were fine. They were for partiers and heroin was for losers. I pretended I was a partier.

Reporters from New York showed up, smug and awful, terrible actors pretending concern and wanting to talk with queers after the Dahmer story broke. Twice I picked up tricks carrying tape recorders. No thanks. I make my money with my mouth but not that way. It got where I could spot their shoes and the way they were pushy asking my name.

Keenan and I were pallbearers for the funeral of an acquaintance because AIDS had already killed most of his friends. We borrowed absurd little suits from a regular trick. Walking in the church was like stepping into someone's rape fantasy with no safe word. We played along, bowing our heads and listening as people spoke gibberish. After the last solemn amen, we hauled the casket to the hearse, pretended to walk to our nonexistent car for the drive to the cemetery, and bussed home where a fifth awaited.

I see Keenan swagger down the street in his half-distracted way, checking himself out in store windows. Me, trailing, unhindered by beauty, head high, pants tight, ass out, making the best of the available light. A Jesus freak accosts us, and we laugh. We aren't damned because we don't believe in hokey shit like sin and god.

Keenan gone, what, twenty-plus years?

* * *

For a while, Marshall was kept by a man who paid his rent and sent him money like a sponsor child. Then he had an open relationship they ran like a business: a right of first refusal.

Marshall followed Oscar Wilde's dictum that moderation is a fatal thing, and nothing succeeds like excess. He didn't succeed but he did exceed. He loved movies starring actors and actresses in their final roles. "She was dying of cancer during filming," he'd say, sidelong, eyes on the screen. He loved disowning people, ideas, accomplishments—calling time spent on them squandered. "The Lost Years," he said of his time in Los Angeles. I swiped as much of his attitude as I could convincingly wield.

I think of Marshall's thin fingers on the bedspread. Light moves over them as the tree branches outside sway in the wind. Circles of yellowish illumination zip back and forth, and he moves his fingers in a counterrhythm to the light. A twitchy gesture as if the sun tickles.

* * *

Rudy texted that something had happened to Shane. No more information. I found the article immediately online. Shane's body had been recovered from the shore by a bridge. Without saying it outright, it was clear: he had killed himself.

I sat on the steps and cried.

Shane and I had been back in contact, but we were not in touch. Whenever I'd heard from him over the last several years, he was texting some version of "I don't want to be here" from parties, work, restaurants, nightclubs, gallery openings, and holidays. I agreed with him. Most of those sounded horrible. His texts were funny, but I knew he was serious. Accumulated, they showed a man who never wanted to be anywhere, who was looking to leave, then he did.

To have survived, to have started over again and again, then crowning fifty to have killed himself, was cruel. I want to say I can't understand. I want to say it's senseless, but I do understand and sometimes it makes more sense than not.

I looked up the weather for the day Shane died. Sunny. Seventy-three degrees. Sidestep the *No Pedestrians* sign, walk out onto the bridge, the water below. White sun. Silence. Who knows if he steeled himself for the fall, or if it was as natural as the night we slipped out an apartment window onto a rickety fire escape and jumped from the second floor to the ground, landing in the alley imperfectly but raising our arms as triumphant teen Olympic whores? 9.5, we shouted and laughed.

Shane and I were out late. We might have stayed out later and made more money, but the high was wearing off and my last guy had been rough. We cut through an alley and found a man lying on the ground on his side, back to us. Drunk or asleep I wasn't sure. Shane said we should piss on him. I saw the keys in the man's hand. He was in a suit. A nice one. I walked over. Shane lit a cigarette. I nudged the suit with my foot.

"He's dead?" Shane joked.

"I think he is."

"What?"

"He's not breathing."

I crouched down and touched him. Cold but not yet rigid. His eyes were half-closed.

Without a word between us, we emptied his pockets. A gold money clip with close to one hundred dollars. I told Shane to leave the watch and ring. Anything traceable. I handed him half the cash. We returned the man to his side and looked around. I clipped Shane's cigarette from his lips for a quick drag and we hurried out of the alley.

* * *

We were like two chorus girls. Tony shook his hips all over the stage. He had a thick ass, so his shimmy worked, but I didn't so I had to really dance. He ground against me, and we counted the cash afterward.

I met a man who didn't like me dancing and quit to move with him into a little house where I read all day and made drinks when he got home. Tony called a couple times from his new life in Los Angeles.

A year later, I was squatting in a warehouse when Tony visited town with his boyfriend. We met up, laughed and gossiped, and he helped me get well in the bathroom. The next morning, they were back to California.

The following spring, Tony came through town again and I went to his hotel. He smiled big, hugged me tight, and slapped my back. I hoped we'd score. Instead, Tony asked me to pray with him. He'd kicked drugs and was no longer with his boyfriend. He talked about the king of heaven and the marks where the nails had pierced Christ. I thought he was fucking with me. Tony got down on his knees and prayed aloud for my soul. He prayed for me to not use my effeminacy as a shield. I waited for him to finish. When he stood, I thanked him and said I had to go. He looked sad but walked me to the door.

A few years later, Tony died. A mutual friend called and asked me to speak at the memorial. A life celebration. I tried to write something. Scrapped it, got high, and wrote something early the next morning. I took a cab to the airport and made it all the way to the gate before I turned back. I'd call and make an excuse and stay in my apartment getting high. Heading into the light toward a cab, I moved my hips a little extra. Shield up.

* * *

"Well, I've talked so much about my rape my coffee's gone cold," KC said the first time we hung out, and I knew we would be friends. "What about you?'

"I'd sooner die than tell that story again," I began. "Let me make a fresh pot."

KC came to my apartment, sat at my rusted Formica table, drank coffee, and smoked. We called my kitchen the Black Lung Café and talked all morning before heading out to our jobs or errands or back to bed to read away afternoons and kill the February blues. Her thick hands and nimble fingers—lesbian hung, she said. Her squint and glare game made Clint Eastwood look like the pantywaist actor he was. We told stories on who we were and weren't fucking. The ones we weren't always more intriguing for evading us. The soft, sad bi boy batted away by his girlfriend after her abortion. The stuttering semantics major who mooned around the takeout counter at KC's weekend job.

KC, a force taken out by force, a car passed a semi on I-90 and knocked her motorcycle off the road at seventy miles per hour. She lingered in the hospital for three days in a coma. Body taken back to Iowa, "all that goddamn beige and blue" she'd said. Filed in a family plot with her full name stamped in stone. A name no one ever used, and I still won't here.

* * *

"Craig is a bird now," Gabe said. Craig had come back that spring to be with him again. I kept my tongue still and nodded. Gabe was an ornithologist studying only one bird. People talked and worried but did nothing. I brought Gabe dope. Two months later, he said it hardly hurts as the needle went in his arm. It hurts less and less all the time, I said. We became lovers. High enough we didn't have to touch, which was best. Gabe called me the bird's name. Someone offered me a place in Chicago, and I left in a snowstorm. I saw him one last time in a bar. His ebullient smile erased, his athlete's build dwindled, he rambled until he nodded out. I slipped out the back. Gabe died a year later, overdosed on the first day of spring.

* * *

Frank told me, "I don't trust anybody who hasn't been to hell."

I was embarrassed by the words *trust* and *hell*.

Frank talked about suicide pacts while we lay in bed. We were high and killing ourselves in a way, but without a timetable. Drugs made matters such as life and death beside the point. Why did he have to pull my mind back?

"We should kill ourselves."

You first, buddy.

Frank's suicide talk pissed me off. Not because I thought my life was precious or held great promise but because he couldn't do anything alone. Suicide was something I kept as an option—my retirement plan maybe—but I envisioned it as a solo flight.

Years later, drifting up the coast on a farewell tour, stopping at roadside dives, picking up strays like lint and giving away money and some sex, Frank was content for the first time in years. His approaching death made him light and generous with others and, for once, himself. Must be careful, he wrote in a ragged pocket notebook, or I will confuse this for happiness and lose track of my plan.

Afterward, some friends said his death was tragic and asked why. I said I imagined people killed themselves for reasons as varied as the ones others used to live.

Frank left the pocket notebook for me. The attached note said I would understand.

"What did it say?" one friend said.

"It was the portrait of a mind progressing through disintegration."

"Did he mention me?"

I understood perfectly. I understood more each day.

* * *

Henry had been on and off heroin for years. Quit and started drinking heavily. Booze was his new love. Finally dried out, he got hooked on pills. Back and forth for a few years. "I want to die sober," he told me one night. He quit everything and stayed the course until he got his year chip. Happy sober anniversary was the last thing I said to him. During the religious ceremony, I subbed a lot of words: Ye though I walk through the Valley of the Dolls, I will fear no pharmacist because this script is legit.

* * *

Knowing the end was near, William threw a party. Everyone came to say goodbye. Rudy said, "He was as happy as a motherfucker at a PTA meeting."

* * *

I hear Paul's voice:

"I believe everyone is deeply damaged. It's the human condition. Some people just don't know they're deeply damaged. Poor dears, they think they're normal. Imagine being *that* damaged."

"Any place whose inhabitants are referred to as townsfolk scares the hell out of me."

"Are you one of those people who thinks Joan of Arc was Noah's wife?"

"Are you getting a case of the sinceres, dear?"

"I won't play the fool to be loved anymore, so I won't be loved."

* * *

Paul once told me a lot of his problems stemmed from living his life according to a declaration made by Truman Capote: I'm an alcoholic. I'm a drug addict. I'm a homosexual. I'm a genius.

"Well, three out of four isn't bad."

* * *

One of the last times I saw Paul healthy, he stood at the top of the stairs while I hoofed up the three flights. As I got closer, he said, "Come up and pee on me sometime" in a perfect Mae West impression, hip wiggle, eye roll, all of it. Dingy sun from the ancient skylight shown on his flinty blue eyes, buzzed hair, scruff of beard, asymmetrical face. A consummate insomniac with a face that told the tale of many lost nights. He flung open the apartment door with a crumpled expression. "You're late. Get in here."

Televisions were on. One in the kitchen, one in the living room, one in the bedroom. Different movies on each one. Moving between rooms, they became one long, jumbled film. Locations shifted, characters vanished never to appear again. Meaningless, badly edited, bombastic music. Tension simply dissipated, nothing more. An accurate representation of life.

We sat uncomfortably on a couch and chair like a sliding-scale therapist's office. The railroad apartment was bone-white and dusty. Paul launched into a monologue: the litany of hours awake throughout the night, shoulder pain, back pain, stiff joints, mental anguish, racing thoughts, the call he had ignored, and how he wanted a white-noise machine with the sound of rain falling on a tin roof.

"Sounds soothing," I said. "Can I refresh your drink?"

I stood and jingled the ice in my glass. I made myself one and one for him. Both strong.

What he didn't like today, organized in the letter C: consensus, convention, collaboration, commitment. Preaching to the choir or entertaining the troops, who could tell the difference? Paul turned his venom in one long-breathed exhalation to all the processed people moving like meat through a horrid factory, becoming test cases, cannon fodder, cogs, and personnel. He spat the last into a segmented worm of disdain: "per-son-nel."

We drank ourselves silly, then we drank ourselves sad. The stories darkened, grew embittered or became a vast silence, the present and the recent past made no appearance. The tales told were long ago when life had been good. Life was not good now.

I nodded and watched his neglected cigarette smoke itself. He scouted my face and scowled. "You're somewhere else today."

"I'm not sleeping well."

"What are you taking for it?"

"Alcohol, I guess. A meditation class has been recommended to me. Or getting laid. Or dating."

"Try boxing. It offers all the pleasure of being hit in the face without the hassle of a relationship," he said. "I have some sleeping pills that might do the trick."

I didn't say yes or no. I let him get them for me, disappearing into his bathroom and returning with a blank plastic bottle.

"Here."

* * *

By the end of his life Paul was so angry and insulting he'd driven most friends away. Those who remained lashed ourselves to the mast and faced the gale force of his vicious tirades. I found my Nightingale mask slipping.

One afternoon Paul brought me to tears and chastised me. "Stop crying, you've always been too emotional."

I became calm, horribly calm, like the still air before a tornado.

Soon he was complaining again: the room, the staff, the smell, how dumpy all his visitors were dressed.

"What happened to having a sense of style?" he said. "Rise to my occasion."

I was quiet. I looked down at the clothes I'd slept in.

He pulled a blanket up. "I'm so cold and stiff," he said.

Not cold and stiff enough, I thought.

* * *

While clearing out Paul's apartment, I found a box with a note taped to it: *Sex toys: If I died, throw this out. Trust me.*

* * *

The coroner said they found white powder and a pipe and Arlo "had been down" since probably Monday or maybe Sunday. She could tell he'd had heart issues because his legs were blue. She said his death was instant and he didn't suffer. After the autopsy, his body would be taken to the funeral home. "I knew this day was coming. I've known for years," Denny said. I knew too. But why did inevitability have to be so dependably vicious? I remember what Paul said toward the end, his voice a croak, "I want to see how your story goes." That's what I wanted. More. To be wrong. Wrong in a new way.

* * *

The night is a train and people keep getting off and getting on. My father is here, young and handsome and not tired by alcohol and life the way I usually remember him. The train leaves and arrives ten years earlier somewhere else. Faces of dead people appear. I smile and wave. Glad to see some, pained to see others. As they pass, I close my eyes and when they open again it's another year, a different coast. Shane offers me a pull from his hip flask. I look at the monogrammed letters. AR? Shane, whose name is this? Arthur Rimbaud, he laughs. For real? No, no, I got it like that. Remember I was called Arty by that man? Oh yeah. I miss you, he says. I miss you too. I have to go. He stands. The squares of light move across his shirt and his chest changes and I look up at Frank's face. Hi, Johnny, he says. His arm is raised. Hi Frankie. Our ballad. The ballad of Frankie and Johnny. Doesn't Frankie shoot Johnny in that song? Yeah, Frank laughs. He leans forward. This is my stop. He pecks my cheek. I want the kiss on my lips. Can I come too? Frank shakes his head, and the train stops. I watch the way his shoulders bunch and relax, willing him to look back once, quick, but he doesn't. When I look outside through the window, they are all there, lightly waving. I start to wave back, but the train is moving again.

2

Suddenly I'm a middle-aged man drinking coffee in a garage. When I was a teenager, I wanted a completely different face. This morning I looked in the mirror and thought, Congratulations kid, you got your wish.

Rudy told me when he turned fifty, he understood he was going to die. "I mean, I'd known, but this was different. I felt unprepared for how it hit me." He became a stranger in his neighborhood. So many were gone, and he didn't know the new faces and they didn't want to know him. He was an old man.

He'd been smoking since he was fourteen and the climb up to his fifth-floor walk-up was a struggle. "I feel it now," he said.

Rudy was constantly at war with the landlord of his rent-controlled apartment. When his mother got sick and needed care, he took the payout and moved home.

In his telling there were sometimes other factors—the changing city, too many ghosts, a crazy ex—but I mostly thought of his daily uphill hike and him resting on the landings.

Rudy and I talk on the phone late at night, often from one or two until dawn. He lives in New Orleans and I live in Wisconsin. Both of us have returned to our home states after decades away in New York, Los Angeles, and Berlin.

When I was still living in New York, muddling through one sublet fiasco after another, I would call Rudy. "Babe, you have got to get out of that city," he'd say. "When I left, I never looked back." Finally, I gave up on New York and told Rudy about my Midwest plan. He said, "How long have you been feeling suicidal?"

Nearly two decades separate us but Rudy talks like we're peers. "It's not that we're old. It's that we're from another time," he has said many late nights. Sometimes it rankles me and sometimes it comforts me to be lumped in with him.

"We're the last two queens on phones not looking at dick pics," Rudy says. In truth, I exhausted the seizure-inducing strobe of hookup apps hours before, but I play along with Rudy's portrait of us as old maids.

I say I prefer the term spinster because it gives the impression of money stashed in the end pages of books by Wharton and James and Sitwell. The imagined library in a crumbling house delights Rudy. The fact of my tiny barren apartment with its poverty-queen minimalism doesn't intrude, the same as the reality of what separates us—thousands of miles, an age gap, finances—is closed by hours of chatty bitchery and our need to laugh.

* * *

I met Rudy when I was seventeen. He thought I was a girl at first. I had ratty bleached-blonde hair with dark roots, eyeliner, lipstick, nail polish, and a thrift store dress over jeans.

Rudy had a large rundown apartment with heavy draperies and rugs. Days and nights were indistinguishable. He shot high-antifashion photos for money and snaps of junked-out girly boys for art.

Many of Rudy's photos were beautiful—and boring for it. The right light, the perfect angle, the film-still sheen. Some were beautiful in their ugliness. The best were unresolved, beautifully ugly but unfinished. They couldn't decide which to be.

Rudy sent me on errands and let me keep the change. He gave me advice: avoid the games, men are shit, don't ask for permission. So I stole a few little trinkets and baubles and pawned them. I nabbed books. If I couldn't pronounce the authors' names, I assumed they were good. It was my night school.

I posed for Rudy a few times. Dressed up in thrift store clothes and costumes salvaged from an aborted movie production, a mix of pirate and southern belle with streaks of makeup where lips and eyes should be. Rudy was high and we went up to the roof with its questionable areas—don't stand there—reminding me of outdoor ice skating as a kid: thin ice. It was windy and rain threatened. Almost done. Hold still. Hold it. Hold it.

* * *

Rudy talks. I listen but not to the words. I can hear the time in Rudy's voice. Rich and beautiful. The others—the gone—are stuck in their young voices. The lightness. I had it too. Cracked now, worn. Unrecognizable from my breathy girlish lilt. Rudy pauses. "And then?" I say. A guess. He barrels on.

* * *

Brandon meets me because I'm his older friend and he wants to know what is wrong with older men. My answer is the only one I know: Everything.

I find myself, between bites of a ridiculously large sandwich that marks me as some lunch size queen, wiping my beard with a useless paper napkin and telling Brandon, "We were told we had a death wish by people who wished us dead. The generation before mine was wiped out and my generation all thought we would die too. Sex was scary. Intimacy impossible. And now we're older and there's this daddy culture. Everyone's a dad. I'm a fucking daddy. Me.

It's stupid. And it's all accelerated by apps. We're all living like sex tourists through our phones."

"You have something—" Brandon mimes that something is in my beard.

I wipe at it. "Better?"

"It's gone."

So is the steam of my mini-festo. I don't even care to follow these thoughts with more thoughts. I ask about the man Brandon is seeing. This is how I can be of value, listening to the story. I have no advice, only my own damage which I can't be bothered to gussy up as wisdom.

* * *

I can't sleep. I've made my way through half a paperback I read once long ago. A novel written with telegraphic wit in 1970s New York. The author was going to be a big name but never finished his sophomore novel, dragging out its writing into a public performance with many withering one-liners and bon mots. He died in the early '80s, the avant-garde of the plague years. I'm a sucker for those one-off bright flashes who fizzle. Failures and losers and also-rans, forgotten or briefly resurrected by some tiny publisher before sinking again like stones.

My eyes are tired. I glance at the coat hooks by the door with only my coat, hat, and scarf neatly on them. I think of Frank's dirty sleeves, cigarette-ashed hems, frayed collars, and half-broken, snaggled zippers. After he died, I had one of his T-shirts thick with his smell. I fell asleep with him still with me. I woke up in the middle of the night confused he wasn't.

* * *

"Beard check," Frank called.

I got out of bed and walked to the bathroom where I squinted under the bright lights. He wanted me to look at his neck where he'd trimmed his beard line and leaned his head back. I examined his throat and beard.

"Looks good. I never realized how crooked your nose is."

"If I get in another fight, it better be with a left-hander, so it gets straightened out."

He shooed me from the bathroom. Even though we'd been sleeping together for months he always showered alone. I returned to bed, heard the water, his low humming, and fell asleep.

* * *

Frank wanted a Christmas tree. Did we have a tree stand to fill with water and keep the ornamented nightmare on life support? We did, he assured me. Somewhere. He dug for it in storage, and I tried to get in the festive spirit.

My idea was to cut out pictures of Judy Garland's face, adhere them to long tinsel boas, and string the tree: Garland on Garlands. Frank vetoed it in favor of something tasteful.

I looked around at the large photo of a guy jacking off, the umbilical-like twine mobile with its strangely blinking lights, the collection of Morton Salt containers, neon bullets, and framed dime bags, and thought, Uh, sure.

Cruising the makeshift lot, we inspected the small spruces and runty pines until a salesman approached us. "Can I help you?"

"We're looking for a small tree," Frank said, "something with more negative space."

The salesman knit his brow. "What?"

"Like a Charlie Brown tree," I said.

"Oh, over here," he said, leading the way.

Later after we'd dragged the tree back to Frank's apartment, he said, "You acted embarrassed of me."

"I wasn't acting embarrassed," I said.

I didn't say more. I poured drinks and we decorated the tree with tasteful white lights and a few keepsakey decorations I would gladly have thrown out, and we both tried to ignore that the tree smelled faintly of piss.

* * *

"You never wanted to settle down," Frank said.

Settle was a word of defeat. I was defeated but *settle* suggested delusions I couldn't afford.

The final week with Frank was like the last stretch before I'd left home as a teenager. I wasn't wanted anymore. The faces of my mother's disgust and Frank's rage merged.

I hardly had anything to pack. No furniture, my kitchen utensils and dishes were minimal enough to suggest a camping trip. Two bags, coat, scarf, and hat. Like I was fleeing the country.

I looked at my few belongings. *Belongings*—such an odd word.

* * *

"You're still young," Denny says over the phone. But I'm not young. The only person who would say I'm young is someone else my age. Someone who also says frequently they still feel like they did when they were a teenager. I don't feel like I did when I was a teenager. Or a child. Or twenty-five. I don't even feel the same as I did ten years ago. Childhood was sad and confusing, and those feelings only grew with time. I learned to pantomime the elaborate ways other adults attempted to mask their sadness and disorientation. My friends and former friends and acquaintances expend frantic energy to be worthy. I know I'm unworthy. And irrelevant. Not fading but already faded, turning into the stripe of light above my bed as my friend continues to give me a pep talk of platitudes, to wear me down until I say everything will be fine and change the subject to his home renovations and upcoming trip to Rome.

* * *

My neighbors marvel at my minimal apartment. "This is the result of rabid homophobia in the '80s and '90s keeping me in abject poverty and shaping the rest of my life. Would you like some coffee?"

* * *

"Don't let money stop you," Denny says. "Don't let it rule your decisions."

Spoken by someone with money.

"If money weren't a factor," he begins.

If money weren't a factor would mean a life so radically different from this one, these choices would be made irrelevant. Or would they be more like choices because they had the autonomy of money backing them? If money weren't a factor, would we even know each other? Part of our friendship is contingent on imbalance. Denny gets social and monetary advantage and proximity to an imagined bohemianism or unconventional life. I get proximity to stability that reinforces a vague moral superiority. Both of us measure against the other and feel fleeting satisfaction. It lasts the length of a coffee date and a few blocks of walking before the old dread rears up.

* * *

I met Colin when he passed through town. I wasn't surprised to find us all these years later talking about failed relationships.

"I always think I need to open up," Colin said.

"And that thought alone shuts you right down."

"Stops me dead in my tracks."

"And he senses it."

"Yeah, and he pulls back."

"I know. If I had a dollar for every time I've been told I'm closed off, I'd own a castle. With a moat."

"It was all of the things that didn't happen."

"I never know which is worse, the things that don't happen or the things that do."

"One or the other of them kills it."

"I usually kill it myself before it goes that far. I see where it's heading, and I cut my losses."

"Very practical."

"Or cowardly."

We remembered social workers, outreach volunteers, and youth counselors with their advice, programs, groups, condoms, free anonymous screenings, and clean syringes. They trained us to be vigilant. No exceptions. They saved our lives and they taught us to not trust anyone.

We talked about escorting as a positive experience. I said it may have even created my self-esteem. To be an effeminate boy despised and mocked and at sea in his body, then to be adored and paid to bare that body had been powerful. I believed the words as I said them but knew I wouldn't later.

The sky darkened. We paid and left a large tip for hogging a table, even though the restaurant had been mostly empty.

As we walked around, Colin pointed out the place where the porn arcade once stood. "That's where we met."

A mixture of rain and snow had created deep puddles, sopping my leather boots, saturating my light wool pea-coat. Both of us, middle-aged, or not so young as Colin preferred to call us, and still dressed inappropriately for the weather.

I said we should do this more often, knowing we wouldn't, and hugged goodbye.

I walked a few blocks remembering when I was sixteen and Colin had called crying and said, "Andy died."

"The punk kid from the Dunk or Dine?"

"No, Andy Warhol."

"Oh."

We both had loved *Interview* magazine, but I wasn't about to cry over a dead celebrity. Especially someone so old. Nearly sixty.

* * *

The newspaper runs a correction to an article on a movie director: "Because of a transcription error, an interview misquoted him. He said, 'You must leave out the painful parts, or you would never do certain things'—not 'live out' the painful parts."

I agree with the misquote.

* * *

As terms go, spatial anxiety sounds positively expansive compared to agoraphobia.

I'm stuck in my apartment watching road movies. I've been on a Wim Wenders kick. His 1970s road movies—*Alice in the Cities*, *The Wrong Move*, and *Kings of the Road*—and the ones that felt like road movies, or just dislocated, like *The American Friend* based on Patricia Highsmith's *Ripley's Game*. It stars Dennis Hopper as Ripley, which doesn't quite work. For me, Nicholas Ray playing Derwatt the art forger, with his eye patch and craggy deadpan pronouncements, steals the show. "A little older, a little more confused," he says watching Hopper/Ripley walk away. And this: "You're right, I'm dead and I'm doing very well."

Last winter Rudy and I watched Werner Schroeter movies for a month. Our midnight-to-near-dawn phone calls were dominated by talk of them, divas, opera, and fables. The *tableauxjobs* as Rudy called them. Schroeter's muse Magdalena Montezuma. The makeup in the early movies that made the actresses resemble drag queens.

"Pure Ethyl Eichelberger," Rudy mumbled close to 4 a.m. about one such performance.

"Wasn't Schroeter the model for the director character in Gary Indiana's *Gone Tomorrow*?" I asked.

"Maybe. Probably. Who knows," Rudy said, sounding like a Gary Indiana character.

* * *

Rudy says that I'm a stay-at-home dad with no kids or pets, "but you are a queen of a certain age with facial hair, so you qualify."

My agoraphobia is camouflaged by winter. Everyone hibernates so who can tell. In the last week a polar vortex has hit the Midwest with temperatures of forty below zero. I texted Brandon telling him not to go out in severe cold for a hookup. Paradoxical undressing isn't sexy. Online I've seen friends lament their shut-in status and cabin fever, making jokes about *The Shining*. I'm not about to tell anyone that often days, sometimes weeks, pass without me going outside.

Rudy knows, sort of. "You're like Greta Garbo," he said.

But Garbo was known for her long walks of up to six miles a day. I've seen the photos of her wearing her Hush Puppies wandering Manhattan. I've read the quote attributed to her: "Often I just go where the man in front of me is going. I couldn't survive here if I didn't walk. I couldn't be twenty-four hours in this apartment. I get out and look at the human beings." The human beings in New York and the human beings in Wisconsin are a very different look.

* * *

Denny stopped by and dropped his coat by the door, shook off the cold. I served coffee and eased into a chair with masking tape binding it together. I sunk back and leaned, resting my elbows on my knees.

"You need some comfortable chairs. This one is awful," Denny said.

Denny turned any conversation back to himself. Today that tendency was a relief. He nattered on about two men he was interested in and two men that he was not interested in.

"No more three-ways. They just make me lonely and I end up doing all the work."

"You're the scullery maid of cocksucking," I said.

"It was fun, but I started to feel like a whore. I mean, they're a couple and they have all these rules. Can I smoke?"

"It's better if you don't. The neighbors complain."

Denny stood and lifted the window with some effort.

"This should be okay."

I got up, grabbed another sweater, a thin cardigan, and draped it over the shoulders of the thick knit I was already wearing.

Denny waited, smoking languorously with lavish exhales.

"Neither of them would kiss me, and kissing is such a big part of sex for me, so I couldn't stay hard. Then the more I thought about not being hard, the more I couldn't get hard."

"Maybe you need a break."

"Yeah, but I worry. I know guys who take breaks and that's it. Suddenly they're forty and it's over. No offense."

"Maybe you just need a fuck buddy."

"I suppose. It gets too intimate sometimes though, and I really prefer the three-way thing. It's much more fun."

"Well, you probably can't have a three-way and complain it isn't intimate."

Silence hung in the air. Smoke was blown sideways through the screen. Denny stubbed out his cigarette. "Time for my shrink appointment."

3

Shane's clothes were more sealant than fabric—sprayed on, shiny finish. He wore them like the hard shell of a toy animated to life by others' imaginations. I was more like a hologram, a cheap illusion. He told stories about yearning to be tough, scraping his knuckles on cement until they bled, cultivating calluses and rough spots, the pride he took in scars, lowering his voice and moving his mouth less beneath a slit-eyed gaze. We were alike. Both of us shot into the world still marked by our makers like bullets streaked by their barrels. And we had collided.

* * *

Shane had a place and I needed one. I slept on the couch and he took the bedroom, bringing home a train of one-night stands after bar time. I lay awake with one eye shut as they fumbled through the next half hour—stabs of light, burnt smells, water splashing, doors creaking open and shut.

One night Shane brought in a thick, sweet-faced middle-aged man. The man looked at me, then back at Shane.

"How much extra for the little one?"

I went along with it.

* * *

That summer my face organized itself. My lips were ripe. My eyes were bright. I have photos.

In the beginning I didn't think to use a pseudonym. We started turning occasional doubles together. Shane had a car, and I didn't drive. We'd go out and he'd make the moves and do the talking. The men thought I was shy. That was hot. Eventually Shane had me work alone. He still drove me around, so I gave him a cut.

My clients offered advice. Usually, it was to get out of the business.

"I wish you'd value yourself more."

"Do you want to pay more?"

I did value myself. I set a price and it was more than I made bussing tables or washing dishes. I'd finish those shifts with little in tips, exhausted and demeaned. At the end of my pay period, I'd get a check and barely make rent. Turning tricks wasn't so bad. I was treated like an object, but I was an object with money.

It was mostly keeping it up for the ugly and fat ones, but I'd always been able to get turned on by someone else's attraction to me. The power of holding someone in thrall moved my blood. I looked so young I figured I was practically doing a public service. Giving pedophiles a way to blow off steam.

* * *

Shane and I stayed out all night and drove home at dawn with the windows down. My arms were peeling from sunburn. The dead skin moved like tiny flowers in the wind. We stopped and watched the rowers on the lake. Their long, fluid strokes became parts, mechanics pushing them along. The catch, the drive, the finish, the recovery. Legs compressed, braced to push off the foot stretchers, the power of the drive, the way the body hung from the oars by the hands.

I thought I could save us, rescue us from men and money and tight rooms with hard light. I thought we could go somewhere else and change and be together. I pictured us like salamanders emerging from the fire with bright iridescent scales.

* * *

Tricks of the trade, Shane called them. Giggle nervously and look away or down, then back at the john's eyes.

"Older dudes love that shit from little guys like you."

Shane dispensed these street wisdoms and they worked. It maddened me. I wanted less predictability. Why was everyone so perfect to type? But if they weren't, if they threw off the behaviors and codes, I knew it wouldn't be good. It wouldn't be a human moment between us. It would be a monster movie. The hand grabbing the ankle from under the bed.

Shane taught me to haggle in cars, to get forty for a thirty-dollar job, to look away from the young boys. Block it out. You can't change it. You can't save anyone. Third time a guy circles the block, back away and ignore him. Unless it's freezing cold, your stomach is growling, and you're strung out. Then go. So, always go.

* * *

In a hotel room in downtown Madison, a man wore a robe and came in while I stood at the sink in my underwear with shaving cream on my face looking in the mirror at him behind me. It was the same scenario each time. One holiday season he brought a badger-bristle brush and lather and used a straight razor. That got my attention. I was hard at the glint of steel. Not that he noticed. He was lost in the workings of his dream, one he had played out countless times with boys like me and maybe even long ago as a boy like me.

* * *

A friend drove over a thousand miles to surprise Shane for his birthday. This was the height of allegiance, a brother or sisterhood we strove to live. The visitor stood in the living room of the decrepit house, posing in Sunday-morning light, and we gathered around. Tomorrow someone would fuck a friend's man, steal something for drugs, run a scam for fifteen bucks, but today, with the smell of burnt coffee in the air and cigarette ash mixed with slush on the floor, we greeted his odd arrival with love. Lemme take your coat. Lemme get you coffee. Have a seat. Need a bath? A blanket? Are you hungry? How do you like your eggs? Five boys playing mom.

* * *

"Bitter crown, don't be that queen," Shane sang. A made-up song in a surprising voice.

"You can really sing, man," I said.

"Nah." He laughed, dripped beer on a rug, wiped it up with his finger and stuck the tip in his mouth.

Bitter crown, bitter crown.

* * *

Another night, another room. Naked and mad at god because the guy kept saying, "Oh god, oh god." Rapture already and get off me.

* * *

The john sucked my fingers. We smoked pot, which I never liked, and watched TV. I found it pleasantly distracting but looking at the time I decided I wanted to get this over. I rolled onto him and he smiled. An ad played in the background. Suck, suck, suck. "The quicker picker-upper ..." Oh yeah, daddy ...

* * *

Pop a Valium. Keep even. We were in a hotel downtown, a nice one, and I was thinking we'd be asked to leave. No matter how much money our trick had, it wasn't likely such an establishment would tolerate what Shane and I meant. But we weren't asked or told anything. We glided through the lobby's reflecting pools to its smeared metal elevators and were scooped up and taken to another floor. My feet snagged at each step, but I was trying on a smile.

John's eyes and skin were jaundiced. Couldn't be good ... didn't matter. No matter. Matter and energy, that was us. I held Shane's hand. John wanted schoolboys. We had a set of improvisations. Shane went Method, all Lee Strasberg, and I followed. John had whiskers like a sturgeon, bottom-feeding the whole time. Was that all he wanted? Maybe. Probably not. I threw myself out of my body and watched what happened. I was the passenger pitched from the car. I watched it burn.

Everything took twice as long as it should have, but then it was over. Money was exchanged. Shane's hand to his pocket and we hit the door soaring, down elevator, lobby, street. Into the night. We were headed somewhere to make more money or spend what we'd made.

Walking through the cold, Shane and I shared a pair of gloves. He wore the right and I wore the left. I put my other hand in my pocket. Shane's pants were too tight for the pocket to accommodate his hand, so he opened his jacket and tucked it in the lining, looking like a painting of Napoleon.

* * *

The man was dressed in all black except for his strange tan shoes. He talked too much. It worked to cover something up and created imbalance. I told him to go clean up in the bathroom and as soon as the faucet turned on, I grabbed my coat and left.

"Did he seem like a cop?" Shane said.

We sat in a lousy all-night diner with an assortment of human wrecks and Shane stared at his plate of ketchup-sodden fries and coffee, too high to eat.

I nodded but I didn't think so. Cops worried me, they could tangle you up or toy with you, but I was afraid of psychos who'd torture and kill you, disperse you in trash bags along the highway.

* * *

The guy had a slender build and a shock of gray hair. He was like a beloved regional college—small but well endowed. I beat him. I called him worthless, ugly, and stupid. I slapped his face, spit on him, and made him strip. I insulted his cock. I forced him outside onto the balcony and locked the door, berating him. He wept and begged to be let back in. He pressed his naked body against the sliding glass door and shot his load. Afterward he told me I had done a great job and he wanted to see me once a week.

* * *

We shuffled our feet to stay warm behind the arcade. No cars were out but an occasional yellow cab. Everything was still. I jangled coins in my pocket. Shane rattled his keys. We sang our ditty in low voices. *A penny for your thoughts, a nickel for your kiss, why does your pussy smell like old man's piss?*

* * *

The door barely cleared the bed when opened. The room was a closet with flocked wallpaper the texture of old newspapers and carpet like moss and the window faced a brick wall. In that furred claustrophobia a man stood nervously, not wanting to sit down on the bedspread.

"You a cop?" I said.

"No, I'm a salesman."

"Where are you from?"

"No Name, Colorado."

He smiled and loosened up. His shoulders dropped. His hometown was usually a conversation starter for him. No Neck from No Name went on for a bit and I let him. It was his hour. He ran out of things to say, and I told him to get undressed.

"I'm going to the bathroom to take a leak. I'll be right back."

The bathroom was tiny and had a shower stall with a plastic curtain that looked like a used condom. The lighting was sallow, making my bruises pop for inspection. I'd known they were there but hadn't realized how many there were. They were in various stages of blooming and fading.

I opened the door, and No Neck was under the covers. He had draped his button-down shirt over the bedside lamp. Ambience. The bed was spongy, and I straddled him with the filthy blanket between us so I could turn off the other lamp.

"That better," I said. It wasn't a question.

We were shadows and I went to work.

* * *

An old man, with thick flecks of dandruff on his silk robe patterned in black-and-red swirls, told me, "I feel so alone." I offered comfort—for a price. But our whole arrangement said this: You are.

* * *

The dark sky peeked through heavy clouds, lit from below by distant streetlights. The only stars were scattered on the beach towel bunched up in the grass.

"Let's swim!"

Shane stripped off his shorts. His slender legs and flopping cock flashed by as he ran toward the water, his filthy soles flipping up and down.

I was so high. This was all beloved. Everything powdery.

I moved my head and there was my childhood. A basement, a shooting gallery, xeroxed punk-show fliers, dingy rooms. I was back on the beach. I traced the stars on the towel and thought of leaving. That would be something.

* * *

Shane and I teamed a trick. He was huge and sweating. Shane was in a strange mood about the guy. We had him bookended. Shane was behind him, and I stood in front of him, sinking into the mattress and catching awful glimpses in the mirror across from me. My unfocused eyes zeroed in on my face in feigned ecstasy.

Usually for this sort of trick I watched Shane for inspiration, but he was hamming it up, slapping the guy's ass as if he were keeping time. Shane had obviously crossed that line between loosened up and sloppy drunk. He started talking dirty, fake cooing and trilling, "Oh yeah, daddy."

Finally, I cracked, laughing so hard I spit. Shane broke into a grin, then a gust of laughter, until he wheezed. Like a rhino, the trick moved with amazing dexterity, standing up in one motion and wiping his mouth.

"Get the fuck out of here you fucking bitches."

Ha ha ha. Bitches!

"I hope you whores get AIDS!"

Ha ha ha ha. AIDS!

The trick threw our clothes in the hall where we dressed quickly.

"What about our money?" Shane said, dancing from foot to foot as he shimmied into his pants.

"Fuck you."

We cackled and crowed. Everything triggered more hysterics: the buttoned-up passenger on the elevator, the serious night clerk at the desk, a passing police car. Tears streamed down our faces.

4

Marilyn Monroe is on the screen.

"If I'm going to be alone then I want to be by myself," she says.

Marilyn sits at a table at Harrah's drinking scotch on the rocks. Thelma Ritter sits to her screen left with her arm in a sling and a wary expression on her face. Her gaze returns to Monroe, looking at her and beyond her.

"Well, you're free. Maybe the trouble is you're not used to it yet," Ritter says.

"No, the trouble is I always end up back where I started. Never had anybody much. Here I am." Monroe's voice falls a bit at this last line, and she looks at her glass. It feels like I'm pushing against my skin from the inside.

I remember reading that *The Misfits* halted shooting for ten days so Monroe could check into the hospital. The cinematographer said, "Her eyes won't focus."

When the movie ends, I click through channels of commercials for gadgets and cleaning products. A man and woman walk hand in hand on a beach toward a red-orb sunset. Orange-kneed tarantulas are gentle, according to the TV nature program. They move without leaving a trace, like ghosts.

The show I settle on is full of action and sudden shifts of emotion and attitude, but the actress in it remains half-blank. Part of her face is immobile from cosmetic surgery. It's like Alice in her Wonderland with insanity happening to her or around her, but she remains strangely untouchable. The actress tries to convey something with her eyes, but they are only confused. For a moment I think that her performance is brilliant. She isn't a troubled private detective gone too far. She is unflappable, unmoved, a force without consequence that is also a conclusion. She isn't believable, but no one really expects that. She is playing god in this show.

* * *

I was on the beach before the morning fog burned off. Walking through the haze I sensed something watching from a stand of trees, but I only saw the outlines of trunks and branches.

I thought of something Christopher Isherwood wrote in his journals about a trip with Igor and Vera Stravinsky: "We drove up once to the sequoia forest, and I remember

Stravinsky, so tiny, looking up at this enormous giant sequoia and standing there for a long time in meditation and then turning to me and saying: That's serious."

The shore was empty and quiet, only the sound of the water. The beach was like all beaches. They were about standing at the end of earth and being made small. I lay in the sand, closed my eyes, and listened to the soapy advance of the tide, a slow slap as the water touched and touched again, a lazy sadist.

I lay for a long time. When I got up, the fog had receded a little. A red-winged blackbird moved along a branch, closing in on its end. It leaned and fell. Opening its wings, the bird pulled up and swooped out in a quick dark line on the water's surface. Then up into the sky, pulling in the distance and vanishing.

* * *

A story Rudy told once: Peggy Lee in Las Vegas pilled into oblivion. Her strand of pearls breaks, and they scatter. She crouches down, crawls, picking up pearls one by one. An anguished and angry voice from the audience shouts, "You were the American dream!" Her band plays on and on. Finally, she stands and steps to the microphone, enters back into the song, smooth, unruffled. Her hand, a fist of pearls.

Years later, I ran across an interview with her. Decked out in a billowy white gown and many strands of pearls, she said, "I don't like marking time. I like to think of everything as now. Haven't the scientists more or less proven that's true?"

* * *

"They feel the trauma of those times, too. Not firsthand, but it shaped everything that came after," I say.

Rudy is scornful of young gay men who haven't lost anyone to AIDS, who grew up after AIDS became treatable, claiming grief about AIDS.

"They don't know though," he says. "They never will."

I pause and there's so much I want to say, but already it's falling away.

I've wanted Rudy to understand me. He's the closest I've had to someone who does. But when I consider the reverse—am I that person to him? Does he want to be understood?—I see how stupid the wish is. That's what is wrong: it's a wish. A desire for something to happen. The entirety of the phrase floats off. Yearning for Rudy to see the cause, the explanation for my life. It's cruel to want someone to see everything about you because you can't imagine yourself as real.

* * *

Brunch with Brandon and his friends. I listen to stories of vacations, property inspections, renovations, PrEP,

Grindr, marriages. Our server—young, handsome, poised—wears a T-shirt with Silence = Death on a pink-triangle background.

* * *

Another species of defeat: people in their forties who say, "In the end, you realize it's family that's important."

* * *

Everyone at the dinner talked about retirement, about the impossibility of retirement, but even in their talk of impossibility I understood they had savings and plans. I had a medical directive and a will. Those had been my big adult moments. My taking-care-of-business decisions. No funeral. No religion. Cremation or if they would take my corpse, one of those forensics-training programs where they leave bodies in a field to decompose and have students come out and look at them. I would be a learning tool. But did I want to be a rotting thing for study? After a lifetime away from the educational industrial complex, did I really need to be a specimen? I spent most of my fag life not being able to donate blood and in a moment of fuck-that had the designation of organ donor removed from my last license. No blood, no organs, so probably no corpse either. Ashes and a party. Informal. No speeches. People together awkwardly in a room sharing stories and realizing the pieces didn't quite fit together, that I had never been the person they thought. Or had they thought I was a person?

* * *

Rudy tells me a friend of his had a nervous breakdown at fifty. A breakdown? My sense of it isn't that things shatter. It's that the fragments all start to come together and point insistently toward one conclusion. So clearly, I'm still all right.

* * *

The white-noise machine is supposed to be the gentle shush of ocean, but it sounds like the crackling fire of papers burning.

Usually when I can't sleep, I watch foreign movies with the sound turned down, reading the subtitles. Anything with Isabelle Huppert will do. Especially ones where she takes younger lovers. Her silent face orders the world, and soon enough it's dawn. But tonight, I'm replaying bad times, remembering the wrong things: the fights that left me raw, the words that cut me for years.

On TV, cops interrogate a necrophiliac.

Perp: Can I get a glass of water?

Cop: Lots of ice, the way you like it?

I turn the channel to a documentary. Something about war with grainy footage of dark projectiles in smoke, which look like crows in a snowstorm. A man intones more numbers and more carnage is shown. He says: "War talk by men who have been in a war is always interesting while moon talk by a poet who has never been to the moon is often dull.—Mark Twain."

I would rather hear the poet's moon talk. That's always been part of my problem.

* * *

Rudy sends me a link to an article. A photo of remains discovered in Pompeii. "For the first time ever, archaeologists have been able to cast the complete figure of a horse that perished in the volcanic eruption." A comment below the article reads, "Beautiful and heartbreaking." It's neither really. It's petrified.

* * *

I read that ruins are more interesting once you knew who made them. Did *made* mean built or did *made* mean destroyed? Destroyed but not completely. You could live in ruins.

* * *

Rudy tells me about how the artist Paul Thek abandoned his best-known work *The Tomb*, which included a life-size effigy of him, and how it was subsequently destroyed. "Do you know what Thek said when someone asked him why? He said, 'Imagine having to bury yourself over and over.'"

* * *

Last summer I asked Rudy, "Where do you think all the people who called us bitter in the '90s are now?"

"At the Whitney's David Wojnarowicz exhibit," he said.

* * *

Occasionally Rudy talks about some of the models who came by and for flashes of beauty were paid in cash or drugs or both. Many departed never to be seen again. Rudy complains about being used by them. As the night is slowly destroyed by dawn, he rattles off their names and mentions others—friends who have left him. "They all go," he says.

"I'm not going anywhere," I say. I've said it before and I've always meant it in that lazy, sleepless way, but in a larger sense it is truer than anything else I've said.

Rudy ends our night quoting Jane Austen's *Pride and Prejudice*: "Now Mary, you've delighted us quite enough for one evening."

Daylight shows around the edges of my curtains. I forget I haven't left my apartment in a week. I forget the heaviness of my days given over to make-up sleep and the way nights have become elastic and unreal, hours moving through long-gone decades, old hopes and loves shuffling like flash cards, names and images not quite aligning, and the hour before dawn when the pull not to live is strong. I fight it, flexing my old defiance, saving the day I will sleep through. I can't let *them* win, I think. But who is *them*—someone who has hurt and forgotten me, an imagined foe, powerful people, or is *them* who it has always been: everyone who isn't me?

5

Forty moves and over a hundred roommates. Madison addresses alone: Orchard and Mound, Baldwin, Dahlen, Inez Apartments on Johnson, Gilman, Gorham, Carroll, State, Bayview Apartments on University, Jenifer, Bassett. Each name raises a gallery of faces. The rooms blur into one, like a dream where a house opens into another and another, crossing time and space. The same cracked plaster, poor lighting, and lead paint. Another four walls. Better floor. No windows, only a skylight. Like living at the bottom of a well.

I traveled light. One sweater, one coat, two pairs of pants, three shirts, a week's worth of socks. No underwear. Kept my boots clean and shined, cut my own hair, stole books and food. Slept on floors and couches, edges of beds. Not eating for a few days sharpened the mind. Quick, cold showers kicked up the internal furnace.

My survival hung on the conditional kindness of strangers. Women who envisioned themselves as den mothers, older men who fancied themselves as generous and sexy, people collectors, the deeply bored. I was their willing foster child, ward, trophy, jester. I resented them and hated myself as I moved once again with a paper bag full of clothes and a few books. I was a perfect houseguest: a sweet, agreeable lap fag with a smile and a quip for everyone. The nicest guy you'd never know.

* * *

Madison, 1988: I was without a fixed address. Denny told me the French used the term *sans domicile fixe*—SDF—and I tried but couldn't make the term work. I drifted from place to place, excused my presence, my mouth, my mind. Everyone drank too much alcohol or smoked too much weed and asked me the same questions day after day, having forgotten or disliked my previous answers. I lived like a fireman, sleeping in my clothes so I only had to put on my boots to leave in a hurry.

* * *

A boarding house with a shared bathroom and kitchen. The gas stove was missing knobs and could only be turned on with a pair of pliers. The shower door had to be held shut. Pots used to catch leaks in the ceiling were later employed to boil noodles. I slept on a filthy mattress and a yellowed pillowcase covering a lumpy mash.

I was invited to a dinner party. Fortunately, it wasn't a potluck, or I couldn't have gone. I wore my one good sweater and a pair of pants that weren't jeans. I thought I looked adult.

The food was baronial. Plates crowded with meat and greens. Conversation was bright and fast. The wine's warmth spread out and made everyone kind and friendly. I was a little in love with all of them.

Dinner was finished, dishes cleared, coats fetched.

I floated on the night and the wine and someone laughing at something I'd said because I was clever and sweet and *how old are you?* Sixteen, almost seventeen, I'd said over and over. My age was part of the fun.

Back in the boarding house, I padded from the bathroom to my room and thought of the large hands of the man who'd sat beside me at dinner, daintily cutting his food into perfectly square portions. I imagined his arm around me as I lay in bed fully dressed and saw my breath.

* * *

Moving through buildings: apartments that looked like extended-stay hotel rooms, hotel rooms that looked like independent-living facilities, rehabs that looked like youth hostels, psych wards that looked like psych wards. At night,

I imagined my name being called during attendance in my old classrooms. A name I no longer used. Absentee. Sometimes I felt I'd escaped and sometimes I felt I'd been banished.

* * *

Missing-persons posters from copy shops, handwritten and rife with misspellings, stapled and tacked to telephone poles. Strange ones with heart-dotted *i*'s and punctuation marks. *Call home.* Vanished, absconded, disappeared. If I saw one of these kids, would I know the difference? I was in the afterlife of my old name, and I didn't want to be returned. Besides, there was nowhere to go.

* * *

I remember a fight when I was a teenager. My mother choked on her fury: "It's god's punishment! You'll get AIDS!"

I'm still here and she's dead. Cancer is a motherfucker.

* * *

I was on acid in a car with a man whose name was either Jason or Jasper. I couldn't remember. I hoped it was Jasper. Sounded sexier. But as we picked up speed and the road flew out from under the car and broke apart into streaks, I wanted his name to be Jason. Jason with good credit and a family he loved. Jason with quick reflexes and an instinct toward goodness. Not Jasper who would kill us both because what did it matter. Not Jasper with the long-gone dad and the mom who drank and called him worthless. Not Jasper who gave a teenager acid and said, "I'm going to fuck you so hard …" and trailed off because he too was seeing things as they flew past the windows which had come loose and floated away.

* * *

I was on my knees, but the man didn't stop hitting me until I said *more* and *harder*. I knew how to ruin any mood.

I could smell my sweat, but fear wouldn't stop me from stealing the man's satisfaction.

He would let me go eventually because he wouldn't know what else to do.

I knew men were easy. I was one—mostly. Not the right kind, which was why I'd ended up with him. Men who needed to beat the little amount of man left in you. Or maybe they were beating the bitch out. Maybe they were making you a new kind of man. One like them. Fake.

* * *

We stood there, me with the cash in my pocket and him near tears telling me of *all the hard losses of the last several years*—his phrase. I nodded and wondered how much he knew. Enough, but not enough to do much beyond his little performance. I'd outmaneuvered him and he knew and loathed me, and worse yet—and more deeply—loathed himself for having been played.

He said, "I'm happy for you," and opened his arms in a grand bear hug, all heat and size. When he let go, his eyes watered.

"You're the best," I said. I meant it. Of the two of us, he was the better one.

I touched his shoulder and thanked him. I didn't let my guard down as I left the hotel room and walked the long hall to the elevator. Not until the doors closed and I began descending did my shoulders relax. I would take a cab back to my borrowed room. As long as I stayed alone in that room, I would be the best.

* * *

Notches in the door frame at that man's house. Were they from his childhood or did they belong to his foster sons over the years? I didn't ask.

"Tell me about yourself," the man said.

"Too broad," I said. "Ask me a question."

He laughed. This skinny little boy-girl telling him how it was going to be. It wasn't even part of the seduction, the business transaction. That little shimmy was later. This was an attitude borne straight from exhaustion. I was seventeen and I was done explaining myself.

* * *

My mind went away while I kissed him. A welcome sensation, especially if it went far enough away that I forgot where I was and that I was kissing him.

We stopped and reached for our respective drinks. My arm was too close and knocked into mine. The glass wobbled. I sensed his body tighten and relax, tired too.

"I may need to sleep," I said into the lip of the glass as I brought it to my mouth.

He grunted in agreement.

We spent longer getting to bed, turning off lights, picking our way through the mess of the apartment, arranging pillows, and pulling back the covers than we had kissing. Sleep was serious.

He undressed and dropped his clothes on the floor, replacing them with other shapeless cotton shirts and sweatshorts. I'd once told him I thought gray sweatpants were sexy, with the outline of a man's cock in them. I hadn't meant on him. But he stood before me in them now looking smaller and grayer than the clothes.

He was asleep within minutes of lying down.

Leaving was a matter of when. I didn't have anywhere to go. So many moves, so many men: the blurring of the two, indistinct and somehow more forgivable for their muddiness. If they were straightforward transactions, it brought a terrible oldness, a cave I could fall into with a familiar gravity. This had started as one thing and then become the obvious exchange of a place to live for my body and my time.

Now the need to flee was constant, even with drinks, even with a clouded head. I reminded myself of how hard the year before had been, the scarcity of food, warmth, and kindness, and the eviction notice. Then one night I'd found him outside a bar smoking and talking. I asked for a light, bantered, and followed him inside where I revealed the outline of my situation as a quick jaunty sketch that hid the fear. He said he had room. "Come stay until you get on your feet."

Within a week, I knew standing wasn't the position he preferred me in. I made a play, a show, of surrender: what I wanted and what I would give up, measured with a wicked grin. I told myself the arrangement was a setback, and I would work my way free again and leave all of this behind.

Now the nights of slow drinks and trailing hours of numb talk had taken their toll. I imagined places and people. I ran my hand over him. I wanted to survey his body before it became memory, a pin on a faded map I would measure my future distance by.

Yes, soon I would get up and leave. I would dress and close the door. Leave before light. But first I would close my eyes and rest, let the gray of the room go black, for a moment.

* * *

"I'm not going to be your escape goat anymore," Keenan yelled.

I laughed. "It's scapegoat, dumbass."

"Fuck you."

The only thing swift about him was his death.

* * *

Once I'd been a little in love with Kennan. The line between friendship and romance was blurry. Piled in dumpy apartments, I lay in beds beside them awake in bonered agony. I followed them around through their romances, tricks, and screaming fights, and thought eventually someone would understand my devotion and love me. They hadn't noticed, or they had and had liked the attention but done nothing more than bask in it. At some point my love twisted up. Jealousy—*you went home with him, but you won't sleep with me?*—became anger and anger became a slow-burning contempt for the object of my unwanted affection and for myself.

I see Keenan standing at the far end of the room, leaning against the bar to extend and showcase his legs, watching the door where a stream of men appeared in pairs and trios, all pirouetting for inspection, murmuring the flaws revealed by the only good light in the room, directly above the entrance. Him, him, not him, him, not him.

* * *

With Keenan at the second Pride march in Dubuque, Iowa, in 1988. The year prior hecklers shouted and threw rocks and eggs at the 30 marchers. There were 575 of us at this one. It was a march, not a parade. Lots of hecklers. Scary as hell. I was seventeen.

We ended up at a restaurant because we couldn't get into bars, and we hadn't bought tickets to the after-march concert featuring Ferron. The diners glared at my long hair and Keenan's short cutoffs. We had three hours to kill and not get killed.

Keenan was quiet. We didn't talk about what we'd seen. The groups of moms not discouraging their young kids from throwing rocks at us, but rather laughing about it, and several guys hanging out on a small flatbed truck brandishing baseball bats, shouting "Go home, faggots." No smiles, just nerves, and all of us walking straight ahead, not making eye contact with the crowd, wondering when a rock would crack our skulls.

* * *

Friends asked me along when they got test results. After the first HIV-positive diagnosis, I learned to take the day off work and plan accordingly. I might spend the afternoon and night at someone's apartment as the shock wore off and the news sunk in. Often the shock returned, and the process repeated. Plans were discussed, dismissed, and dissected. If the news was good—negative—we celebrated at the Plaza or Jocko's. We laughed and talked. I still thought about lost wages amidst the relief, about working a double or tricking to make rent.

* * *

Did we talk about our families? A little. We were queer and we were out on our own. Not much more to say. It was obvious.

Kennan's mother had been unstable and bent to frequent emotional breakdowns—meltdowns, he and his brother called them. "Here comes Three Mile Island," they'd say.

Shane's father caught him in bed with another boy and beat him badly, cracking two ribs and breaking his nose. Shane left and never looked back, or so he liked to say. But with a few drinks or a little weed he'd tell and retell the story.

KC's father loved reading Western novels. She remembered him throwing one across the room once. "They killed the horse, goddammit." He found her stash of dyke pulp romances and burned them and changed the locks.

Craig, two years older than me but somehow infinitely older, was an orphan. His mother stories were sweet and sad. We'd drive around, nowhere in mind, smoking and talking. "Take the long way," I'd say and listen.

* * *

Fifteen. I went to the office of the school superintendent. "There's no money for you," he said. I'd attempted suicide a few months earlier, transferred schools, and transferred back. I'd called the Hetrick-Martin Institute in New York City, begged to attend the newly opened Harvey Milk High School, and been told only city residents could. I'd run away, been arrested, been returned. I looked at him, considered the steps to his desk, the cheap brass letter opener, his neck, prison. I walked out. I never returned to school. Won't even vote in one.

* * *

Appleton, Ashland, Evansville, Sheboygan, all of us with the stories of our beatings and humiliations and the teachers and administrators who didn't care or encouraged it. Kennan's science teacher joined in. Marshall had internal bleeding from four boys kicking him in the second-floor bathroom of his high school. Their stories brought up my movie and the poisonous rage only cigarettes and drinks quelled.

* * *

When I discovered Gena Rowlands was from Madison and Milwaukee it gave me hope. A genius of performance came from my place. She escaped. She washed the Wisconsin out of her speech and carriage. She lived.

Willem Dafoe played Jesus in that Scorsese film. I remember the uproar, but I couldn't bother to see the movie. I'd had enough of god shit by then. Dafoe, who grew up in Appleton, told a glossy men's mag, "You gotta leave Wisconsin behind when you're playing Christ, right?"

6

An insomniac tells himself the dreams he isn't having. Black dice with the white spots worn off. You know they were there once. The dimples count but you must pay close attention. Squint and focus. Your vision isn't good enough for that. Roll the dice and make it up. Winning and losing.

Is Pluto still a planet? Is Saint Christopher no longer a saint? I quiz the ceiling. I'll sleep when I'm dead. Am I dead yet? I'm awake in a floaty half state. A pageant of bad decisions takes the stage. I lie in bed tabulating my crimes and regrets on some imagined yet powerful abacus. I number the dead friends and the living friends and think where I should be filed. Where I fit. Neither column.

Sleep is unfaithful to me. I'm living one long day striped by darkness. I close my eyes, which are burning with fatigue, and try to empty myself for sleep, but it never comes. Instead, Paul's face: yellow, distorted, his eyes filled with fear, his mouth open and struggling. Lips stretched over teeth, eyelids fluttering, nothingness in the big pupils, then milky, closed. Rattling breath. At each, I wondered which would stay with me, if one thing would comprise my last image of him, but it's all of them, moving like a carousel.

* * *

Denny tells me he never thought he'd own a house, get married, adopt, and yet he has. He never thought he'd see forty. He's now fifty. I hear this the way I have in the past with a shrug of yes obviously, a shrug of yes me too. Except I don't own a home, I'm not married, I don't have children, and I'm not yet fifty. I don't want any of those—house, husband, child—and often I don't care to see the other side of fifty. This has all been enough. Too much really. The generosity of life's disappointments has been sufficient.

* * *

Rudy says our ancestors didn't sleep for eight hours straight. They slept in three-to-four-hour periods. He wants me to shake labeling myself an insomniac.

"It's negative thinking. A negative label."

"Negativity is my strength. I'm a man of my word and that word is usually no."

* * *

Discarnate, adjective: (Of a person or being) not having a physical body. "Only when he moves does he appear frail and birdlike—discarnate."

I can't remember certain voices. I see the face, the walk, the way they smoked a cigarette or raised a glass. A silent movie.

I didn't understand the phrase *dead and gone*. "He's been dead and gone over a year," people said. It was redundant. But now I understand the slack time between dead and gone. Shane is dead but he isn't yet gone. Others are gone. Some return and go again. Like the living.

I pick up a book on the stages of grief. A little paperback to help tidy the mess into neat dimensions and appropriate interlude.

The stages: denial, anger, bargaining, depression, and acceptance.

I am great at the first four.

* * *

When people fret about not being where they think they should be in their lives, I hear Paul whisper-lisping "How fucking square."

* * *

"If you were to die this evening with no opportunity to communicate with anyone, what would you regret most not having told someone?" Rudy says.

"I forgive you."

"Why haven't you told them yet?"

"Because I haven't forgiven them."

* * *

Tony talked me into a medical trial study for a liver drug. The money was good. We were in a small room at a cheap folding table with fake woodgrain reading the rules and stipulations: two overnight stays, blood draws, tests administered. I had trouble focusing on the words. Looking at the blank line for my signature, I pictured a locked ward. I stood fast and my chair tipped over.

Tony's hungover eyes widened.

I bailed and called him later. His voice was flat. I rambled, tried to explain without telling too much.

"You're crazy," he said.

I hung up.

* * *

Rudy has a bronchoscope and a colonoscopy scheduled for the same day.

"When I said I wanted to be spit-roasted, this is not what I had in mind."

* * *

Rudy says Truman Capote died in Joanne Carson's arms after giving her a key with no numbers on it. Supposedly to a safe-deposit box. Maybe holding his last manuscript, *Answered Prayers*, the long-rumored and hyped burn book of his rich socialite friends. Others claimed the book didn't exist or they'd seen it but leafing through discovered a Missouri bankroll—a few typed pages on top with blank pages beneath.

* * *

"Insomnia is torture," Brandon says. "Seriously, sleep deprivation can make you crazy."

He has information: vitamin D in fish oil, magnesium citrate twice a day, and three milligrams of melatonin at bedtime. "They should have it at that health store by you. The yuppie-hippie one."

I pause, pretending I'm writing all this down.

"And try rubbing lavender into your feet."

"Unless it's cut with morphine, that's not going to work."

* * *

I'm not interested in meditating to empty my mind. I've already lived that. I grew up with people who hated thought.

* * *

I think constantly about how my desire was tied to death and how much I believed I wouldn't live to be forty. I don't talk about it. No one wants to fuck that story.

* * *

I had no idea anyone would use the term *upstanding member* and not be talking about a hard-on. "As an upstanding member of the LGBTQ community ..." makes me miss a lot of dead and terrible people. Where are my monsters?

When I hear the word *community*, I think of the stoning scene in Shirley Jackson's "The Lottery." I wasn't looking for community. Community was a group of people figuring out how you didn't belong.

* * *

Dead men whose lives are described as "brief, incandescent" or "short, hard." Me, listening and not listening now to these men being proclaimed, wistfully remembered, and yet, still, sometimes turned into tyrants of appetite for loving cock.

* * *

Remember the world before comment sections beneath online obituaries? I miss that.

* * *

I don't believe in luck, other than marveling at what could have gone wrong and didn't, and I don't believe in fate, other than if what goes wrong keeps happening it will create a pattern which necessitates a certain type of resolution.

* * *

Frank flipped through old punk and blues records. He put on Skip James's "Motherless and Fatherless." The voice was keening, high and lonesome, different from when Skip sang "Devil Got My Woman." Something haunted him here. As we sat and listened, drinks in hand taking the edge off, we knew what he meant.

Lord if you see my mama will you tell her to please pray for me?

Tell her I'm way up here in Washington just as sick as a boy can be.

Frank sat with his eyes closed. Everything was different from what I'd hoped, but I could move from here and see a time when I wouldn't need anything. Hardly an epiphany though. I had it each day. A ritual of acceptance lasting the length of a song and a fast-downed drink, turning the past into a haze so it couldn't hurt me.

* * *

Rudy texts at 4 a.m. You awake? Soon we're on the phone.

"The Mama's Boy tattoo across his back was the tipoff but I was all about putting down payments on regret that year."

I talk about my biggest regret.

Rudy says, "That sounds like remorse."

When our conversation ends, I look it up. *Remorse* is defined by *Merriam-Webster* as "a gnawing distress from a sense of guilt for past actions: self-reproach." Gnawing distress.

Well, hello remorse, we were never formally introduced.

* * *

I flip channels. Cop show, SWAT show, FBI show, serial killer show, live active-shooter news footage. Shows where rich women yell at each other. Shows where tattooed people yell at each other. Shows where pundits yell at each other. Shows where addicts yell at each other. Shows where drag queens yell at each other. Combination yellers.

I stumble across *Flamingo Road* starring Joan Crawford as Lana Bellamy, a carnival dancer who ends up in prison, having a conversation with another inmate.

Inmate: You never did say what you was in for.

Lana: They said I was trying to pick up men on the streets. How about you?

Inmate: My boyfriend cut himself on a knife I was holding.

I pull the covers up, a book falls to the floor, and my neighbor coughs. I'm glad to be here and to be alone, but I do wish someone would refill my water.

* * *

Rudy tells me dying in his sleep has been his fear since he was a kid. Really? After all we've seen. Not waking up beats all the other options to me.

"Well, you spent a decade trying everything to not be awake."

"Is that why I can't sleep now?"

"Maybe."

"Fair enough."

* * *

I remember sleep. It was like death but shorter.

Time doesn't heal, but my 4 a.m. comebacks to decades-old putdowns are stellar now.

Somewhere it is the end of the night and people are dancing their last song.

The sun will rise soon. Dawn is evil. I already know the contents and the dimensions of this room, and I do not need sunlight to tell me something different. The bureau, drawers open at odd angles. The desk demanding attention, neglected and judgmental. The bed where I lie, its own universe, contracting slowly.

I read somewhere that between four and five, when it's not night any longer but it isn't morning yet, is the hour of more suicides than any other. Thursdays are the most frequent day of the week. Something about it being before the weekend. Don't worry, it's Tuesday.

* * *

Andy Warhol said people are either beauties or talkers. I've known people who were both: beautiful talkers. I'm a talker, not a beauty. The problem is that as I get older there are less people to talk with. I'm a talker growing ever more silent. Then what? Beauty? I can't afford it.

* * *

Jack Walls on Robert Mapplethorpe:
Robert liked sex and sex agreed with him.
I liked to sleep in the same bed with him at night.

* * *

In artist Jack Smith's last role in *Shadows in the City*, he says, "No kidding folks, they love dead queers here." While filming, Smith was late and his usual impossible self. People told the director, "You want Jack Smith. That's Jack Smith."

* * *

Summer 1989: Rudy took me to see Penny Arcade perform at P.S. 122. She did a monologue from *I Was a White Slave in Harlem* by Margo Howard-Howard, the grand drag queen and embellisher. Jack Smith was in the audience. Up front in a wheelchair. The show concluded with Arcade chopping onions under blue stage lights, talking about the death spiral of downtown New York. Smith died a month later.

* * *

I read an article in the *Los Angeles Times* about an exhibition of matchbooks from now-defunct gay bars and sex clubs. A time that is an intermittent blinking on some abandoned shore, maybe. I relate to this. Sewers of Paris, Basic Plumbing, the Meat Rack, the Big Banana, the Fallen Angel, and Dude City.

Truman Capote on Stanley Siegel's talk show: "We all know a fag is a homosexual gentleman who has just left the room."

Gore Vidal once said, "There are no homosexual people, only homosexual acts." I always found the statement funny. Not because it was an absurd idea. Not at all. It was funny because Gore Vidal was such a faggot.

* * *

I read an obituary of George W. S. Trow. "George had a laugh that was like an explosive device, the kind that in a 1930s movie would make people drop monocles into their soup."

* * *

Shane and I swam out as far as we could. It was either die or swim back to shore. The late-summer water was rougher than we'd anticipated. We sat on the beach shivering. When he stopped shaking, Shane stood and waded back in.

I watched him and calmed down, looking at the waves and the sky until I forgot everything. I hoped death was like that, minus all sensation and thought and light. Afterward, we rode home elated.

7

Arlo overdosed and was taken away by ambulance. His boyfriend Joe said he woke up in the night and found Arlo on the floor unresponsive, blue lipped and barely breathing.

I'd been there before. I awoke one night to the bathtub running over and Arlo submerged. I fished him out, beating him and yelling his name until his eyes opened. He was mad I'd fucked up his high. Once I returned from work and found Arlo on the kitchen floor with a needle still in his arm. I slapped him until he roused. The next summer, he overdosed again. Multiple doses of Narcan revived him. He was in the hospital for a week with heart problems. When his heart found its rhythm, he was sent to jail, then a halfway house, then he lived in a men's shelter until he met Joe at a meeting.

Where was Arlo now? Joe didn't know. I called the ER and hospital admitting. I spelled Arlo's name and gave his date of birth. He wasn't there. Not at the coroner's either.

I called Joe back and said, "Maybe the EMTs cleared him and being that he's on probation, they took him to jail?"

"That's right, he's on probation."

* * *

A crowd stood across the street watching the Hotel Washington burn. The hotel contained four bars, a coffee shop, a barber shop, a restaurant, and hotel rooms, many filled by drag queens, musicians, people who made art, and people who talked about making art. A few of my coworkers lived there, eating meals from room service, watching bands at one bar, drinking at another, playing pool, and taking strangers or repeat offenders back to their rooms. It was rumored one queen hadn't left the building in years, but now I saw her on the curb, bare faced, clutching a thin robe.

Henry came over and hugged me. Around us people cried and stared in disbelief. The fire was mesmerizing, licking away at the three stories. A burst of flame showed in another window and another. Everywhere. The firemen dragged coils of hose back and forth in a futile dance. The water pooled and froze on the ground.

A lunatic waving a handmade sign with a Bible quote jeered at the crowd. "That's your eternity," he yelled.

"You might want to get that Christhole out of here before something happens to him," one of the queens told the startled dyke cop who intervened, moving him to another corner of the street.

We watched until the hotel was gone. Some walls stood like the façade of a war movie set on a Hollywood lot. Henry nudged me along and we moved to a bar where a football game played on multiple televisions. Some eyes showed shock and raw fear. Others hinted that this day was another in long, sideways lives running out of back roads. Maybe they saw it in my eyes too.

Morning turned to afternoon, then dark. We moved locations to the Crystal Corner on Baldwin and Williamson. Some people were still in bathrobes or in borrowed clothes or coats provided by the Red Cross. I drank to the point where I couldn't stand easily. The news came on and we watched ourselves on television. People hushed the bar chatter. TV telling the story meant it mattered. People cried on-screen.

When the news went to commercial, everyone was momentarily energized by the official version. A few minutes later, the mood shifted. The news sealed the story. It had happened and was over. On to sports and weather. Clear and cold tomorrow.

People ordered shots. I looked around. We were bound by this time and event, but we would be townies competing for jobs in a college city in February. I was already thinking of rent and old regulars to call.

I wanted Henry to take me home. Not because it would change anything or become anything. It would provide the voice that had woken me with news of the fire speaking to me the next morning, so life wasn't random fragments. An electrical wire ran through it if you knew where to look and could sense tiny powers.

Across the bar, Henry's hands moved along a man's back. He tilted in and rested his head on the guy's shoulder. Probably best.

Through the glass block window, I saw the lights of a cab idling at the curb outside. I had no reason to leave and no reason to stay. I picked up my coat, not even attempting to navigate my arms into the sleeves. It smelled like smoke. I headed for the lights.

* * *

The letters were stamped in red: *This is from a Correctional Institution*. They arrived like a séance, but filled with boredom, hokery, and meandering philosophical rantings in Arlo's scrawled handwriting.

"I'm writing large. I'm in the dark to some degree. You're the easiest person to write to yet I put it off. I get to a point where I don't write any more. Sometimes it's easier not to think of the outside world. Try to focus and get shit done here. It's been foggy for two days now. No movement due to visibility. If the guards can't see us, they can't shoot us."

Included with the letter was a visitation form.

My favorite question: "Have you ever been in jail or prison? If yes, why, where, and when? (List all—use additional sheets if necessary.)"

I lost track of how many jails and prisons Arlo had been in over the years. Oshkosh, Chippewa Valley, Dodge, Kettle Moraine, Oakhill, Waupun. He went from trouble involving booze and motor vehicles to trouble involving forced entry and weapons, crossing over from criminally stupid to stupidly criminal.

The last letters came from Fox Lake for battery, disorderly conduct, and probation/parole violation. I forgot what the probation and parole originally stemmed from. He was arrested for illegal trespass and parole violation during a police sting at a motel. Public intoxication, DUI, possession, driving without a license. His arrests tended to be compound affairs. Why stop at two charges when you could add resisting arrest for a hat trick?

After Arlo got his third DUI and had a breathalyzer installed on the ignition, he kept the gas tank full. He'd park his truck behind the bar and leave it running while he went in and had a few after his alcohol-education class. Only once did he lose track of time and come out to find the truck dead. Occasionally, someone would come in and say something about a truck running, but most people kept to themselves. Eventually, Arlo totaled the truck and spent three months in county jail. He found a new bar in walking distance of his apartment.

* * *

Arlo said he was from Spread Eagle, Wisconsin, or French Lick, Indiana. He'd used Jackson Hole, Wyoming, for a while but a surprising number of men said they knew someone there. The point was to be cute in bars with names like Rumours and Shenanigans. There was a bar we nicknamed Skankz with a *z* "like Liza" I said, playing up to our audience of old queens. I didn't like Liza or Judy or any show-tunes shit. Musical-theater fags with their maudlin far-off misty eyes as they belted along to some god-awful songs were an occupational hazard but an easy mark. The references brought focus. The distant look honed in. Some man would buy me another drink. Free drinks, places to stay, cash, meals.

Arlo talked about moving south. Atlanta or New Orleans. Thick air and slow talk.

"I need some sun on this ass," Arlo said.

"Yes, you do."

Arlo mooned me as our host walked in with his shirt undone flashing sagging man tits and rippling belly.

"Am I about to get a show?" he said.

We laughed and made out for a bit before turning our attention to him and the money.

* * *

Arlo's first arrest was for solicitation. It was a joke.

"I look so skinny in my mug shot," Arlo said.

"That mug shot is your *Butterfield 8* weight."

* * *

Things got darker and weirder. Arlo went from a person I spent time with to a person I saw to a person I heard about. He smoked crack in various hotel rooms where he set off smoke detectors and overran bathtubs and stained carpet with messy half-eaten takeout. He bragged about a sugar daddy and showed me a gold chain he'd been given. He was leaving us all behind. He'd hit the big time of whoredom. Good for him, I said. The others said he was lying, or he'd be back. We were already divvying up his regulars.

* * *

A Yelp review of Manhattan Central Booking: "Two stars because I've been to clubs worse than this with a longer line, and the car was returned unscratched. Thank goodness they didn't find what was under the tissue in the cup holder."

* * *

Arlo called to let me know he'd been moved to a minimum-security prison. A guy with all gold teeth had smuggled a

Snickers candy bar on the bus, ate it, and proceeded to suck his teeth for the two-hour ride. "If I weren't already in jail…"

* * *

At the guardhouse, five different signs said skirts must be at least three fingers long. I filled out a form with Arlo's prisoner number, handed over my identification, checked my wallet, phone, and jacket in a coin-operated locker, changed out a twenty for quarters, and took off my boots.

After I passed through the metal detector, my hand was stamped like I was entering a nightclub. I walked from the guardhouse to a low brick building where the visitor room looked like a heavily guarded cafeteria. All the food was from vending machines. I was assigned a table beneath a mural of a smiling family.

Outside, I saw Arlo crossing from the other unit. His limp was more pronounced than usual. He appeared at the door and smiled. He waited to be buzzed through and checked in at the desk. I stood and we hugged. There were two fading bruises on Arlo's jaw. I wanted to ask but I knew better. These visits were a careful balancing act. The wrong subject could piss him off or quiet him into a sullen funk.

At the vending machine, I perused the selection and was disappointed they didn't have coffee. The previous prison had coffee and the guards were much friendlier.

They also had games and cards. Neither of us played but it had appeared to make people around us happy. Less family squabbles

I bought us two diet sodas, cheese puffs, and red licorice whips.

"Surprised they let you have whips in here. Potential weapon."

We joked and gossiped about celebrities and TV and movies. He asked how I was, and I lied. He showed me the same courtesy. We switched to a topic which never tired us: men. Men from the past. Men from the now. I talked about a guy I'd been dating, and he talked about a man he worked with in the kitchen.

We ran out of steam before our time was up. The awkwardness at our table wasn't what unsettled me. It was the silence at another table where after years of visits there was nothing left to say.

* * *

Arlo's left knee bounced. He was impatient with other people talking and only wanted his own story now, the same one he'd been telling over the last few days.

When he first called, he was fresh from a stint in the psych ward, which came on the heels of a three-day disappearance. His account lacked specifics. He only said that he'd driven around seeking sleep.

"I like rundown motels," he said.

I didn't say, what else could you afford?

I nodded along, thinking Arlo needed to get the story out of his system and tire himself, but with each subsequent retelling the performance hardened. A little more bravado added and a little more reality subtracted.

I thought Arlo should return to the hospital, but I knew he had no insurance, and they wouldn't hold him for long. I didn't doubt things might end badly, but I thought it could be at least postponed. Our old connection, frayed as it was, pulled me to try, even as I knew my incompetence.

Arlo jiggled and talked too fast about the night of his hospital admittance. Somehow a friend, Powell, who Arlo referred to only by his surname like a junior varsity sports team player, talked Arlo into going to the hospital.

"Powell went into the hospital first and negotiated on my behalf."

Arlo made it sound like an FBI fugitive surrendering.

"They didn't get me in a gown. I stayed in my street clothes."

I didn't say most psych wards let people wear their own clothes. I didn't say they weren't the insane asylums of popular imagination from fifty years ago, but more like corporate cafeterias staffed by plump men and women in pajamalike scrubs. I didn't say I had firsthand experience.

Arlo said he had been given his own room. No roommate. And the staff had never gotten him undressed. "I wasn't going to let them see my meat."

The story skittered to his release. This brash break for his independence was told with his spine erect and his chest out.

"I told them I didn't belong there, and they let me go."

I knew that wasn't right, but I knew it didn't matter.

Once Arlo had returned to his empty house, he'd called me.

"It's hard for me to ask for help."

I looked at the floor. He hadn't asked for help so much as issued a list of demands: he needed cigarettes, groceries, and gas money. The last couple of days had been long, and it promised to be a long night with me sleeping on the couch covered in dog hair. Arlo was glassy with the telling, with some hero's journey. He was working his way into the future one more telling at a time. Future, hurry up already, I thought.

* * *

Things got bad. I ran out of stories.

I borrowed a car and made my way north along the county and back roads. As I drove, I pictured the musty cabin and the rowboat tied to the dock. I saw how I would take the boat out, uncoordinated but determined, finding a slow, sloppy rhythm. In roughly the middle of the lake, I would stop and watch the sun come up. I would slip the tip of the gun into my mouth and squeeze the trigger.

The picture lulled me as it had for weeks, giving me peace in the chaos of the long sleepless nights when I thought of the mess I had made: old grudges, disappointments, love squandered, love rebuked. And the voice that said again and again I had outlived myself.

At the lake cabin, it rained for days. A heavy downpour alternated with drizzle. I couldn't take the boat out. The gun looked dumb and dangerous, like a rebound romance. The picture of the boat at the center of the lake and the rising sun took on the aspect of a bad oil painting, not knowing enough to be campy, only dopey. I was humiliated that even at the end of my life I couldn't make another picture. My dull imagination couldn't find a new way to live or even to die.

I read and listened for the rain to stop. Late afternoons, I drove to a tavern and three times in two days, I heard men bitch about spearfishing rights and throw around slurs. The place was frozen in time, twenty years ago, thirty years ago. It wouldn't matter what else happened in the world or didn't, these men and men like them would always sit in taverns—different songs with the same twang, different taxidermy, different posturing— and talk this way.

I realized if I died on the lake someone would say a faggot shot himself in a boat.

Maybe I had torpedoed my life, but that didn't mean I had to drink pissy beer and eat dusty popcorn alongside morons.

I left the bar and packed at once. I didn't look back at the lake or the docked rowboat as I drove off. I was dazed with the strange hope of someone who'd avoided playing their own hand. Now what? Go home and tell no one. Push on and don't think about it too much. Make up something to tell myself.

8

Fifty. Jesus.

My birthday is so close to Christmas it's always been overshadowed by Jesus the birthday hog. Since childhood I've received joint birthday and Christmas gifts. Years ago, I abandoned my birthday because people were frazzled. They had family celebrations, work parties, and countless obligations. My closest friends were usually broke. In letting go of my birthday, I also let the importance of other people's birthdays fall away. Even children. I simply didn't care.

Once Denny threw his birthday party, renting out the back room of a restaurant, where he presided like royalty over the menagerie of his friends sitting at a long table. Gifts were laid out. He wobbled with one hand over a shiny looped bow as if he were playing a theremin. He opened it—a book—and grimaced. The giver launched nervously into an explanation. A gift with a story was always bad, but I was sorry for the guy as his voice trickled off.

Denny expected more from his birthday than I did from my life.

* * *

I'm in bed reading E. M. Cioran's *The Trouble with Being Born* when Rudy calls.

"Welcome to curmudgeonhood. Have a seat. None of us stand here," Rudy says.

The birthday wishes have come in, mostly texts, but two cards arrived. The idea of me with an address is signal enough of age.

"Happy jubilee, my queen," Eli texts. "A half century of excellence."

I'm crying, not because I'm sad. Or not just sad. Not because I'm old. Not because it's a privilege to be alive when many others are gone. I'm crying because I'm remembered. And that's all there is.

* * *

"You're now open to different wisdoms," the healer says.

Her voice is soft, intimate, like a winter night with a little too much wine. I am close to sleep.

Rudy paid for this, said he thought it would help. A gift—how could I say no? Now lying on my back hearing open your eyes, open your mouth. The healer says she is pulling out negative energy from my throat.

"All that is unsaid, all that you can't speak. Now I will push positive energy in with my right hand."

I don't believe any of this, but the quiet room is welcome. All I have to do is lie here and have energy I can't see or sense pulled from me and replaced. It's a performance, like playing three-card monte in the park. A distraction, harmless within its narrow experience. Find the lady, find the lady, I can hear the man say, moving the cards. I could watch the cards move forever and never pick.

"Your heart needs healed."

Her left hand moves over my heart. Her right is placed over her left as if there is too much to contain. A wave. Find the lady, find the lady.

* * *

Eli called from a road trip in the Trans-Pecos region of West Texas looking for locations where Wim Wenders shot the movie *Paris, Texas*.

"This place is psychedelic in its relentlessness," Eli said.

I pictured Eli back when we were seventeen, looking like a baby dyke Bob Dylan in the sixties. "I don't consider myself outside of anything. I consider myself *not around*," Dylan told a journalist, building his cryptic-oracle Huck Finn persona.

Eli talked about Sam Shepard, who wrote the *Paris, Texas* screenplay and whose book *Motel Chronicles* was a bible for us when we were street kids hitchhiking from Milwaukee to Chicago and New York.

"Did you tell me Sam Shepard wrote a story on a roll of a toilet paper in jail?" Eli said.

"No, he wrote about Genet doing that, secretly writing a novel on toilet paper, having it destroyed by a guard, and then starting it all over. Not sure if it's true."

"Not that it matters. Real or not."

"Not at all."

We talked about that first half hour of *Paris, Texas* when Harry Dean Stanton wandered the desert and didn't speak. His face was the only narrative, really the only story needed. The best lines were his wrinkles. Eli said Allison Anders, who directed *Gas Food Lodging*, had worked on the crew of *Paris, Texas* and run scenes with Harry Dean Stanton. The actor was frustrated because Wenders wouldn't tell him what was on his character's mind during his silent pilgrimage. What is he thinking? Stanton asked. Anders said, Well, when I was fifteen, I was in a catatonic state and I wrote a poem about it. Dean Stockwell was standing there listening and said, Little lady, do you have that poem with you? I do, Anders said, it's back at the hotel. They retrieved the poem, and Stockwell and Stanton questioned Anders about her experience. So that's how Stanton built the interiority of Travis, a laconic middle-aged drifter: he filled himself up with the mind of a catatonic fifteen-year-old girl.

"Really, we all should," I said.

Eli said, "I think we have."

* * *

Beached on the bed. Tonight, I hate what I've created. I feel like my mother. I think about dead friends and aging and that I should get a broom and take care of the cobweb in the corner of the ceiling, but also *Charlotte's Web*.

* * *

Life is narrated at both ends by a birth certificate and an obituary. A tidy beginning and a bow-tie ending.

* * *

"It's about loving yourself. You have to love yourself," Marshall said. "This disease is about shame. It is shame released into the body."

"It's a disease. It isn't feelings. It doesn't care how you feel."

"You don't know what this is like."

"You're right, I don't. But you're committing suicide and calling it something else."

Marshall put his care in alternative medicine and healers. Strange drinks, exclusion diets, crystals, candles, chanting.

He died anyway. Insensible, hallucinating, in horrible pain. Later one of the healers was indicted for fraud.

* * *

We donned our death duds and walked to the church. From the church to the bar. From the bar to my dealer. From my dealer to home. I stripped off the suit, sat by the window, and listened to my straight neighbors laugh and drink in the yard. The smell of meat on the grill. As if the world weren't collapsing.

* * *

Nameless. My type that year was guys who looked like FBI wanted posters. An aesthetic which guaranteed mixed results. We shared a birthday, ex-boyfriends, and bad habits. I would see him on the same block where I scored drugs and we'd ignore each other. He had a penitentiary swagger. It was easy to picture him walking across the exercise yard. His mouth hardly opened when he spoke. One night I went home with him. I didn't see him again after that. It was as if by fucking he vanished. Another mirage.

* * *

I can't repel ghosts when I don't even believe in them. And yet they are everywhere. My nightly jump with memories: the ripped knees of Shane's jeans after we were tossed from a bar that no longer exists and has been replaced by a high-end purse palace stripped to brick and tin, bleak with elegance. Piss-elegance, as Paul used to say, his sibilance more loose with the late hour and cheap beers. Cross the street and one block over, the shiny apartment building with a doorman was a restaurant where I worked with Brent. He moved to Appleton with a friend, then alone to Black River Falls, then rehab and a halfway house in Minneapolis. Finally, moved into the dead column. Classic exit: relapse with a fatal dose, uncertain of what he could tolerate after being clean. Word came weeks later, overheard by Denny in random bar chatter. Denny phoned the next morning to deliver the news. Brent and I weren't close, but he was always around. Some people you know as part of the scenery, a constant presence you take for granted.

* * *

Eli asked me to play a vengeful ghost in their short film and I was both flattered and typecast.

* * *

That winter Frank kept the suicide hotlines busy. He tried not to call more than once a day but when he had to, he called different ones. There was a remarkable amount of them. He called the general ones and the gay ones and the addict ones. He skipped the god ones.

After Frank died, a friend of his said, "Tragic—all the misspellings in his suicide note."

* * *

Chet Baker Sings was on endless play at KC's place. She wanted to look like Chet Baker. She was doing a damn good job. She had two girlfriends who she treated badly. She was being a man. I understood. I stayed with men who hit me. I didn't act straight, but it was hard not to be straight in your thinking.

One night after the man I was living with had finally passed out and the urge to murder him had lifted, I uncurled my hands and called KC. Your face, she said when I opened the truck's door and the interior light came on. We rode in silence. No music.

* * *

KC was on a roaming trip. *Let's get lost.* They found a virgin forest called the Lost 40 with huge trees hundreds of years old. An old-growth pine forest due to an error that occurred during the Public Land Survey in 1882. The pines were missed by loggers because surveyors mistakenly mapped the area as Coddington Lake. The lake is located a half mile to the southeast. The site was surveyed again in 1960 and the error corrected. The forest was incorporated into Big Fork State Forest and its old trees preserved.

* * *

Last spring, I sat in a café and heard a motorcycle. I thought of KC, pictured her pulling up in her leather jacket without a helmet. A guy walked outside and greeted the motorcycle's arrival. Returning inside, he said to the rider, "I know the sound of your engine." That's my idea of true friendship: I know the sound of your engine.

* * *

A few years ago, I went to a cabin with friends for a long weekend. It rained day and night and we ended up playing cards and drinking all the alcohol in the place. The rain finally let up early morning on the day of our scheduled departure. Despite a ragged hangover, I pulled on clothes and boots and went for a sluggish walk on the main road. Down past the bend by some train tracks, I spotted a lean fox as it left the road, not looking back.

I want to place Shane in that weekend, but he wasn't there.

He's strongest now in all the places he was supposed to be. The last time he visited New York and I was still living there, we made plans and he stood me up.

It was the last weekend of the Louise Bourgeois show at the Guggenheim. I went alone and wound my way through the throngs of tightly packed people moving up and up the rotunda spiral past sculptures and installations of nests, traps, cocks, and mother spiders. The further uphill, the tighter the crush of the crowd became.

At the top of the exhibition, an infant let loose with a full-lunged cry that opened and widened, rising into a scream. People bristled, their backs straightened, but I thought it was perfect and satisfying, as though the coiled energy in my torso, which had sapped the heat from my hands and feet, was finally released. My mouth loosened and when the baby stopped, I looked at its flustered mother with gratitude. *Thank you, thank you.*

* * *

Rudy tells me he never believed in eternity until the hospital vigil for Paul. "I don't mean I suddenly got god. I mean dying is a lot of work and waiting for death takes forever."

"I don't want to die," Paul said repeatedly when he was sick.

"I'm not ready to go yet," he said on his deathbed until he lost his voice.

* * *

Paul bestowed advice in mentorly bursts punctuated by cigarettes. I remember them still:

If someone says you're adorable it means they're never going to fuck you.

When someone says you're gifted, they want something for free.

Remember, the goals you set today are tomorrow's disappointments.

Bitter is what stupid people call you when you won't tolerate their bullshit.

When a contrarian says you're wrong, feel flattered.

Opinions are not like assholes. I rarely find opinions pleasurable.

* * *

Rudy once told me if he had to cry in the night he got up and sat the edge of this bed. He refused to cry in his pillow lying down. After Shane died, I only allowed myself to cry in the shower and I turned the water to cold.

* * *

You know when you have the first notes of a song stuck in your head, but you don't know exactly what the song is and as you hum the notes aloud, they turn into another song replacing the fragment and the longing to be completed? A strange melody, a fragment, powerful and relentless and brief and sung over: Shane.

* * *

What Nina Simone does not have in the song "Ain't Got No—I Got Life": home, shoes, money, class, skirts, sweater, perfume, bed, man, mother, culture, friends, schooling, love, name, ticket, token, god. What she does have: hair, head, brains, ears, eyes, nose, mouth, smile, tongue, chin, neck, boobies, heart, soul, back, sex, arms, hands, fingers, legs, feet, toes, liver, blood. I have also lacked everything on the ain't-got-no list. Some I still lack, but I do have a bed now. As far as the got list: I don't have hair or boobies. My smile is intermittent lately, and the jury is out on my soul.

* * *

Heaven. There's a thought.

Reincarnation is cruel. A do-over, practice-makes-perfect way of living, then living again. No thank you. Life eternal. It does sound like a threat.

As a kid in church, I sat and listened to the sermon. The minister said, "Jesus suffered and so should we. It's for our perfecting." I looked around. The congregation nodded. These people are nuts, I thought. My faith was gone by the age of fifteen. I felt totally conned.

Sweet oblivion. The Rapture. Salvation. Those words threaded through my childhood and boiled over in my teens. I let my mother's mind turn into a yellowing Bible pamphlet. Colin used to collect them. The illustrated flipbooks of the damned who never saw the light. Drunk on Mickey's Big Mouths, in the house behind Red Letter News, we intoned the passages to each other and laughed. "Scabies, rabies, and babies," Colin chanted at the end of our recitation and made the sign of the cross on my forehead with beer before letting out a loud belch.

My mother wrote me once: Lord, how many times shall I forgive one who sins against me? Up to seven times? Jesus answered, I tell you, not seven times, but seventy-seven times. I choose forgiveness.

I thought, That's only because you don't want to do math.

* * *

I have forgotten so much that it resembles forgiveness.

9

A journalist called Rudy. "I could smell it. The guy wanted
that rubbernecking sociopolitical sad shit. He kept asking
me about dead people. He asked me: What was it like
being gay in the 1980s? I told him: So much cock. All
kinds. Cock, day and night. Cock around the clock."

Interviews with Rudy are featured in several of those
books about downtown New York. I was impressed Rudy
didn't rehash the same stories over and over again. The
way he disrupted the myths.

I fall into the nostalgia trap sometimes, yearning for
something I imagine was more authentic. All of it ten
years before my time. Rudy says it was another world,
both more and less real than this one. Once I told him I
wished I'd been old enough to see it. "You'd be dead then,
babe," he said.

* * *

Rudy tells a long story about a man he dated briefly in New York.

"I think he was from Superior, Wisconsin," Rudy says. "Is that a place?"

"Yes, it is a place, and it belies its name."

In New York, I missed the horizon. In Wisconsin, I'm exposed and vulnerable, easier to pick off.

Sometimes I forget my Midwestern translations: "You do what you think is best" means "It won't work but go ahead and waste your time."

Why do we live here? I mean all of us and I mean anywhere.

* * *

Rudy shuffles his stories: He had a disastrous affair with a couple in LA ("It wasn't called a throuple then," he says, "I was just a great piece of ass"), sold Black Beauties in Washington Square Park, abandoned his apartment in Berlin to the street kids he photographed. "I don't remember the order," he says. "As John Ford once said, Print the legend."

* * *

Rudy lost track of how many funerals he attended. "If you told me over a hundred, I wouldn't blink."

He tells me about the clubs, piers, brambles, and baths. He lists the bars: the Anvil, the Mineshaft, the Ramrod, the Cockring, the Toilet, the Glory Hole, and Crisco Disco.

"I stopped going to funerals and went out at night, snapping photos high and drunk. Everyone that was left looked like a gorgeous zombie. I couldn't take my eyes off them."

After six months, he haphazardly selected some of the photos and printed them for an upcoming gallery show he could barely care about. It was a hit and became his first book, which made him demifamous. He became known as a Method photographer, living amidst what he was documenting. His relationship with those photos and that book has ebbed and flowed between hesitant embrace and petulant disgust over the years I've known him.

He showed me photos of him and friends at Laguna Beach in the mid-'80s. "Fourth of July?" he said to himself. "David, Jason, and Steve." I didn't ask and he didn't say.

* * *

The sun transforms common objects into eerie, hard masks. White walls blaze with light. The hair on my legs stands up, then I do, like something strange growing into place. Maybe this is what I should be. With many gone and no generation like a stand of trees blocking my view, I can see my own death from here. It's a quiet clearing, perfect and welcoming.

Last night, talking briefly with Denny, he said anything can happen.

Anything can happen is one of those phrases completely about intonation. For a long time, the words hummed with promise. Then, in the way something terrible is sudden, they took on the growl of threat. Now they have the monotone of resignation. The words no longer hold promise or threat. A shrug. Is this acceptance?

* * *

Didn't I let go of this anger long ago? Then I realize, my anger didn't disappear, I was high for a decade. Rage was my savior. I was furious at myself and my malefactors. The excoriating fire cleansed me, left me raw, wounded, yet stronger. Old thoughts gone. Old ways destroyed. I had to fill up with new thoughts, new ways. Push forward.

* * *

Lining the thin pen tray in my desk drawer: KC's stilled pocket watch, Shane's dull pocketknife, my mother's ribbon bookmarker cut from her Bible, and my Saint Dymphna medal. Dymphna, the patron of sexual abuse survivors, runaways, epileptics, and the insane, is my sort of saint. I'm covered and understood by her purview.

Hang the Saint Dymphna medal and my mother's ribbon on a nail in the wall above my desk. The nail was driven in the brick long ago. It isn't going anywhere.

The medal lays across an old bent Jimmy DeSana photo, a self-portrait of him bathed in red light, adorned in a corona of aluminum foil. I think of Saint Joan hearing voices and ending in leg irons, recanting her recantation, her prison time longer than her crusade. I think of her ashes thrown in the Seine to prevent the cultivation of relics.

* * *

My fantasy is heavy blankets and someone bringing me tea and morphine when I ring a little bell. I wear a knit cap and a hooded sweatshirt with an oversized grandpa sweater in an oatmeal shade like a dingy bathrobe. The steam heat has two settings: cremate or meat locker. I can see my breath. I may as well smoke to lend it some heft.

I fetch my emergency pack of cigarettes and layer up. My winter look is basically Patty Hearst as Tania holding up the Hibernia Bank, minus the wig—which may be my mistake.

On the way outside, I pass the old man from the second-floor apartment talking with the building super on the stairs. "All around me they're going. This one heart, that one cancer. And I think each day is precious, but this goddamn winter needs to end."

* * *

The slack week between Christmas and New Year's is like bardo, or some other time when what you do doesn't matter. The end-of-the-year accounts are already closed, and you can't harm yourself further.

Light moves across the wall where the plaster cracks in three places and threads out into spidery lines like a weak pencil drawing.

Snow falls and white dusts the yard, covering the bicycles and trashcans, and furring the upper lip of the Virgin Mary statue in the neighbor's yard. I flick off the lamp and watch the perfectly calibrated descent like a snow globe in need of a tinny windup soundtrack. I'm content to be inside alone, making one up.

* * *

Rudy calls early. He has a party later, he says, though he may not go, but if he does, he may stay late, or leave early and pass out. Either way, he won't be calling me.

We talk about people we know, people we knew, disappearances due to burnout, domesticity, class differences, and grief, the way people want you to be better and get on with things.

"They won't tolerate a moment's breath. Anything that isn't about money and connections is a waste of time," he says, warming to the topic with gleeful disgust.

"Remember when Ed's boyfriend died and he didn't snap right back? People dropped him. They were embarrassed for him."

Ed was inconsolable, sullen, and often drunk. I'd visit and we would fool around as we often had, but he was distant, automated, yet he didn't want me to leave. I wrapped around him. The body of his youth faint beneath his aging, like a drawing covered in layers of tracing paper.

I tell Rudy I should make some dinner. We hang up and I call a takeout place around the corner. My fortune cookie says: "Opportunity is knocking at your door—answer it tomorrow." That's what I like, a fortune with procrastination built in.

* * *

After much cajoling and bitching, last year I visited Rudy in New Orleans for a week. The house was as promised, old and well appointed, filled with antiques and all of Rudy's treasures and junk from decades of thrifting and travel. We drank and smoked and never went outside until the sun set. I pictured my early retirement, stationed on his veranda in a caftan, saying, "I never quite met the right one, and besides I don't like wearing jewelry."

* * *

Thick drawing paper, grid notebooks, charcoal, colored pencils, and the sturdy Parker pens once manufactured in my hometown line my reader's desk pushed against the wall beneath a photo of Joni Mitchell's *Hejira* album artwork I crudely altered, turning her black-clad ice skater into the Grim Reaper.

Winter 1989. Rudy, Shane, and I took a road trip from New York to Wisconsin.

"Flat-ass nothing," Rudy said from the passenger seat, as Shane drove with maniacal focus, chemically jacked on trucker speed. We got lost—*detour*, Shane snarled—in Ohio where a paper plant made the air smell like a fetid fart. Even so, we made good time.

In Madison, Rudy recognized Lake Mendota where Joni was photographed ice skating in a black dress and shawl. "I loved *Hejira*," he said. He told us the title referred to Muhammad's flight from danger and regaled us with Joni Mitchell trivia about the album. She'd taken several road trips in 1975 and 1976 and wrote songs about them.

"Wisconsin was one of the trips?"

"No, I'm sure she was playing a show here. She must have had professional obligations," he sniffed.

I took Rudy to Ella's Deli where I'd once worked briefly.

"Shel Silverstein was one of my customers. His daughter went to the university. He was beautiful and really kind," I said.

I'd served him matzo ball soup and stuttered out my love for his books and the songs he wrote.

"Songs?"

"Yeah, he wrote 'A Boy Named Sue.'"

Rudy tried to convince Shane to stage a photo of *Hejira*'s skating Joni, but he balked. Shane said he couldn't stand New York anymore. He was staying in Wisconsin and had to meet a man about a place. I acted surprised, though I'd overheard him on the hall pay phone in our hotel.

"I can ice skate," I said.

"If there's time tomorrow."

Shane stood us up for breakfast and Rudy skipped the photo. I played a Marianne Faithfull cassette as we left for Chicago. "The Ballad of Lucy Jordan" came on.

"Shel Silverstein wrote this," I said.

As the song faded out, Rudy switched to the radio and searched for an oldies channel. The Supremes came on midsong and he blasted it. *My world is empty without you, babe.*

* * *

The last time I saw Shane, we closed a bar and went back to the place he was crashing. All night, I'd watched him and thought of a story from the set of *The Misfits*: observing the dailies, Clark Gable said of Montgomery Clift, "That faggot is a hell of an actor."

Shane handed me a glass and put on some music. He held a cigarette like a dart. Crushed-out butts lined a saucer sitting on the side table. Speaking slowly, savoring each pause, he was into stories about his old man. "That son of a bitch always said I had million-dollar hands and a ten-cent head. He wanted me to be a baseball player and I could bat something, I tell you."

I wondered about his million-dollar hands and what their street value had ended up being. Shane put his hand on my back. I turned and he looked into my eyes and said nothing. He put an arm across my shoulders and pulled me closer. We'd survived many things together or at least in proximity to one another. To Shane's way of thinking, we'd done so because we were tough and brave. Street smart. To me, our survival was owed to our insignificance. We had slipped through situations because we didn't merit attention, let alone ruin.

I kissed him and he pulled away, first with his body, then with everything else. He excused himself to the bathroom and I sat alone.

When we'd met, I'd thought Shane was smart, but now I understood that he was a little less dumb than me. I needed him to be smart because then it meant I had been led astray.

I found him asleep with his head rested on his arm and his legs at a strange angle. He wore one sock. I pulled the blanket down over his naked foot. He shifted in his sleep, pushing the covers back, revealing the whiteness of his beached body, the splayed limbs with faded tattoos and a new addition that looked ripe to the touch.

Back into the living room, I opened the window and huddled the sill, smoking. My eyes watered. Crushing the cigarette out on the ledge, I considered waking Shane before I gathered myself to go home, but thought, Let him sleep.

* * *

Cleaned the apartment, made it orderly and lemony. Books are piled but reasonable. I need more shelves. Everything is alphabetical by author though I could pull nonfiction off the shelf and tell you the Dewey Decimal number—813.54—a remnant of my years as a public-library autodidact.

I usually say *self-taught* or that I dropped out after eighth grade and left home. The last time I used *auto-didact*, someone said, "You can suck your own dick?"

"No, but my life provides ample evidence that I know how to fuck myself."

In a stack, I found a favorite—Amelia Earhart's *Last Flight*. I bought the book at a library sale when I opened it to the date-due slip on the front page. Unstamped: no check outs, no returns.

Publisher's blurb: "Informal, gay, filled with the spirit of high adventure, this is Amelia Earhart's own story of her great flight, nearly around the world, which ended in tragic disappearance somewhere in mid-Pacific."

My father mistook my childhood obsession with Amelia Earhart for an interest in airplanes. He got books from the library, and I sat with him and listened while he talked about the aircraft in the photographs. His eyes were dreamy. He was back in the service. My own interest in Earhart had nothing to do with aircraft. I only cared because of her disappearance and not because I wanted the mystery solved. What had happened to her wasn't my concern. My concern was that she had vanished and stayed gone.

The book's dedication:

TO FLOYD

with gratitude

for all-weather friendship

I flip to a favorite passage, marked with a ribbon: "Not much more than a month ago I was on the other shore of the Pacific, looking westward. This evening, I looked eastward over the Pacific. In those fast-moving days which have intervened, the whole width of world has passed behind us—except the broad ocean. I shall be glad when we have the hazards of its navigation behind us."

* * *

"The world treats me terrible," Rudy says, half-joking, half-pissed.

It's true. The world treats everyone terrible, whatever the world is. But what have any of us ever done for the world, except show up and expect to collect our inheritance for being born?

We have been on the phone for hours.

"I'm fading," I say.

"I suppose I am too."

How many more times will I talk with Rudy, or watch dawn after a sleepless night, or remember my friends who are gone?

I used to look at photos to see the past, but now I don't need external references. I have my mind dredging up images and stray words I have excised and arranged to form an arc from there to here. That's one way to create the illusion to go on. I know I'm my own maker and unmaker and that knowledge is all the grace I will ever know. I try to find some still spot in all this tilting. Stop moving, I tell myself—the walker, the tightrope, and the distance to the ground all at once.

Sleep comes fitfully. I drift off only to wake and see ten minutes have passed. Finally, I get up because I'm not going to sleep. Fog has settled in, erasing the city and wrapping the world in white. For a moment, I think I may have died.

I dress and walk downstairs.

On the street, I remember an older man told me once, "It's possible to turn into a ghost while you're still alive." I heard the words the way one hears anything like that at eighteen years old—as an old man's self-pity. Wasn't that what most of culture was? He'd paid me for sex, and I was attuned to the performance of listening. And the money. But now I know what he meant—self-pity, sentimentality, transaction, and all.

A door opens and I hear a man's voice. "Wow," he says into the white. He fusses with a bike locked to a street sign's pole and rides off, disappearing.

I'm alive. Of course I'm alive.

Acknowledgments

Parts of this book appeared in different forms in *Catapult*, *Fugue*, *New World Writing*, *SELFFUCK*, *SPUNK*, and the anthology *Little Birds*. My thanks to the editors who published them.

My gratitude to Hedi El Kholti, Chris Kraus, Robert Dewhurst, Eileen Myles, Emily Hall, Richard Porter, Matthew Stadler, Patrick Kiley, Derek McCormack, Kate Zambreno, Olivia Laing, Jeff DeRoche, Erik Moore, Phil Campbell, Katie Kurtz, Chris Fischbach, and John Lippens.

ABOUT THE AUTHOR

Nate Lippens is the author of the novel *My Dead Book*, a finalist for the Republic of Consciousness Prize. His fiction has appeared in the anthologies *Little Birds* (Filthy Loot, 2021), *Responses to Derek Jarman's Blue* (Pilot Press, 2022), and *Pathetic Literature*, edited by Eileen Myles (Grove Press, 2022).